"Whether you've
Orleans to life. I
unraveling myste
food and culture of the city."
- Allison Leotta

PRAISE FOR LAURA CAYOUETTE'S OTHER WORKS

THE SECRET OF THE OTHER MOTHER:
A CHARLOTTE READE MYSTERY

"Laura has an amazing grasp of what New Orleans is. I could
smell it! And that's a good thing!"
- John Schneider

"This book is a trip to New Orleans--not a tourist trip, but an
intimate journey to the heart of the city and its colorful,
exuberant people. If you love NOLA, this is the book for you. If
you don't know NOLA, this book will make it come alive for
you, and you will fall in love. The setting is vivid and
wondrously wrought, and it's just the beginning. The novel
brims with interesting characters and an engaging mystery to
boot. I highly recommend this book."
- Jennifer Kincheloe

LEMONADE FARM

"I've read Laura's novel *Lemonade Farm* and can attest to its
power. It evokes the 1970s in a painfully accurate way, and is
beautifully written. She manages a wide cast of characters and
somehow paints adults, teenagers and children with equal skill
without ever condescending to any of them. Her skill at
characterization and turns of phrase, coupled with a great sense
of place, makes this a heck of a novel."
-Tom Franklin

KNOW SMALL PARTS:
AN ACTOR'S GUIDE TO TURNING MINUTES INTO MOMENTS AND
MOMENTS INTO A CAREER

"Laura's outward beauty could have guaranteed her much more in this business perhaps even worldwide fame. She could have taken an easier route for her professional pursuits but instead chose to make it about the work and only the work. She is a role model in that regard and a true leading lady. Enjoy what she has to say and see if you can see yourself in her journey. She still has some big important parts to play."
-Kevin Costner

"She's nailed the daily life of an actor in L.A. about as perfectly detailed as it gets... You can say that Laura is amazingly correct in everything she says and sees, but she makes you hunt for the urgent need to do it which is at the bottom of all."
-Richard Dreyfuss

"Laura Cayouette is a working actress that also has a happy, well-balanced life. Figuring out how she manages this feat is certainly worth a read."
-Reginald Hudlin

"Anyone who has met Laura knows that she is unforgettable. Perhaps even more impressive is that she has found a way to translate this personal charisma and life-force into her appearances on screen, making the most of every second of camera time given to her. She has literally figured out a way to bottle lightning. I'm sure that her observations and guidance will be invaluable to the actor who is looking to make his or her mark in the film world and to build a career, moment by moment."
-Lou Diamond Phillips

ALSO BY LAURA CAYOUETTE

FICTION

The Secret of the Other Mother: A Charlotte Reade Mystery

Lemonade Farm

NON-FICTION

Know Small Parts: An Actor's Guide to Turning Minutes into Moments and Moments into a Career

How To Be A Widow: A Journey From Grief to Growth
(editor only)

Airplane Reading
Contributor

LAtoNOLA
blog - latonola.com

PREFACE

In an effort to capture the unique culture of New Orleans, many of the people and places mentioned in this fictional novel exist in reality. As such, you can trace Charlotte Reade's steps and enjoy many of her experiences for yourself. In an effort to entertain, I've sometimes bent these real people and places to my fictional will so "real life" experiences may differ.

I have included an Appendix listing many of the restaurants, tours, people and events mentioned in this novel along with links to their sites. For more information and photos on anything mentioned in this book, use the search tool in LAtoNOLA (latonola.com), the blog upon which many of the book's recollections are based.

I've also built a playlist of music videos and videos of parades and other events, places and people included in this story on my YouTube channel:
https://www.youtube.com/user/latonolawordpress

You can link directly to the playlist at:
http://buff.ly/2qwJZUR

And I've created a clipboard of photos on Pinterest:
https://www.pinterest.com/latonola/

Enjoy!

Special Thanks
to
Brenda Bruno
Samantha Shevitz

Extra Special Thanks
to
Bryan Batt
for allowing me to have some fictional fun
with his name.

For "The Three Wise Men."
Quentin who told me to write it,
Ted who read every page as I wrote it
and Andy who supported me all along the way.
Thank you.

LA to NOLA Press

© 2017 Laura Cayouette

ISBN-13: 9781545162538
ISBN-10: 1545162530

First Edition: April 2017

Back cover photo by Robert Larriviere

Many of the people and places mentioned in this fictional novel exist in "real life." At times, the author has bent these real people and places to her fictional will. Although the author has made every effort to ensure the accuracy and completeness of much of the information contained in this book, we assume no responsibility for errors, inaccuracies, omissions, or any inconsistency herein. Any slights of people, places, or organizations are unintentional.

THE HIDDEN HUNTSMAN
A Charlotte Reade Mystery

Laura Cayouette

Chapter 1

The chainlink-fence-lined park was crowded with people selling homemade jambalaya and cupcakes, kids playing football, babies on blankets, neighbors visiting and teens flirting. People wandered past Mardi Gras Indians with their beaded and plumed suits laid out on display in the grass. Friends and family helped the Indians affix the giant, finely beaded panels that told stories mostly of warriors killing fierce animals or other foes. There was no way I was going to be able to capture all of this in a blog.

Tom led me to the gate and we waited for the Indians to line up. "It's a local tradition honoring the Native Americans who took in runaway slaves as members of their tribes. Super Sunday's when all the tribes come out to show off their suits they spent all year makin'. The suits can weigh over a hundred pounds and cost up to five grand. And they can take up to a year to make. They battle over who's the prettiest." He pointed his sweaty go-cup of beer to a dozen guys walking our way. "Uptown tribes make mostly two dimensional suits. Downtown tribes do three dimensional suits and use more rhinestones." His beer moved toward a guy in a mask wielding a feather-trimmed spear. "The Spy Boy goes in front. He's like a scout to tell them if any other tribes are approaching." He was smiling and looking down the line of color-saturated plumage and intricately beaded works of artistic storytelling.

Tom had told me some of this before but repetition was the key to memorization, something every actor knew, and I wanted to know the Mardi Gras Indian traditions inside and out.

"The Flag Boy uses his flag, which are now mostly Chief Sticks, to communicate between the Spy Boy and the Chief. Then between the Flag Boy and the Chief is the Wild Man who keeps the streets clear."

"Sounds like a movie crew. A million specialties and communication is key."

"Yeah, you right."

The gate was barely wide enough for the plumed panoramas to pass through. I snapped photos as fluffy ostrich feathers tickled my ankles. It felt like being kissed by a cloud. Then the chanting began. Though two brass bands led the procession, the Indians played only percussion instruments, like Native Americans, as they sang about sewing, about warring and about not bowing down.

Beyond the allure of the music and the insanely gorgeous suits, there was something beautiful about this through-line from the first culture of America to the present. And there was something beautiful about the creativity and indomitable nature of those slaves, dragged from their own culture, passing down some customs and heritage of those with whom they felt kinship.

I couldn't help but happy-cry taking it all in. I felt like I might fly apart, like I was spilling over with joy from the beauty that survived all that pain.

A few years ago, my father's mother told him that we were part Cherokee. The math worked out to me being one-sixteenth Native American. That was enough to make my dad eligible for a casino, if I wasn't mistaken.

I knew nothing of that heritage, was taught none of those customs. I didn't know the language, the food or the values and traditions that governed my great-great-grandmother's life. Maybe she would have been happy to see that her mixed-race children went on to share the "American Dream." Maybe she would weep for all that wasn't carried forward.

Tom led me to the neutral ground for a better view as more tribes started arriving from down the street. I zoomed in for a shot of a female Indian pushing a decorated stroller filled with a fully-costumed sleeping toddler. Then I looked to the crowd on the curb across the street. "I think I know that guy."

"The one in the Saints jersey?"

"Very funny." There were always dozens of those. "No, the guy with the expensive boy-band haircut."

"Good Lord."

I laughed. "I know, right? I told you a lot of the grown men in L.A. have fussy hair. But that is him. I'm going over."

"I'll keep our spot."

"You sure?" He nodded and gave me a peck on the cheek. I smiled and waved as I walked away. He was already buying his third beer from a guy selling out of the back of his pick-up.

I knew Ethan from a film he'd produced when we were both starting out. They had cast a bigger name in the role I went in for, and I was pretty bummed not to get the part because I wasn't famous enough. Especially since I knew the director. But it beat not getting the part because I wasn't good enough. They'd filmed the whole movie, and Ethan and the director watched the first edit and loved it. Until the end. They agreed the movie needed a happy ending. And they agreed that it should be a girl. The story goes that they turned to each other and said simultaneously... "Charlotte Reade." From then on, they had a nickname for me.

"It's my happy-ending girl!" Ethan's arms flew open.

"Dude, people are going to think you're pimping me." I hugged him quickly and he kissed my cheek. "What are you doing here?"

"Pre-pro on an indi. Working those incentives."

"I know, right?"

"Hey Todd." He slapped a guy near us on the shoulder. "This is Charlotte Reade. She was in the first movie I produced."

Todd put out his hand. I couldn't read the tattoo on his knuckles. "So you lost your virginity together?"

I took his tattooed hand in mine and shook it.

Ethan corrected, "No, it was my first but I was excited because she'd already been in a couple big movies and I would be her first indi."

"So you were a dirty whore slumming." He smiled. They laughed. I was back to having to be a "good sport."

I smiled. "So you guys are crewing up? Let me know if you need any recommendations. I've worked with a fair bit of crew here."

Ethan put his arm around me and I wondered if Tom was watching. "Charlotte is one of the most connected people I know. Random stuff too - movie stars, athletes, politicians, authors, inventors, venture capitalists."

This felt like too easy a set up for another whore joke.

Todd laughed nervously. "Damn, I guess I should watch my mouth with you."

"In general, it's a good idea with any stranger. But don't worry, I grade on a curve. You're okay for now."

He slapped Ethan's shoulder. "I like this chick. We should bring her in for the party scene. We need a feisty older..." He quickly switched gears. "A sophisticated socialite with sass."

Ethan smiled at me. "It's a small part but it could be good."

Another small part. And this one was in a small movie. But it was work. And it would make my new agent happy. "Sure. I'd love to come in. Sounds like fun. And seriously, let me know if you need to know about crew or local actors. I gotta go back to my boyfriend." That felt good to say. I looked to Tom but he was chanting with the Indians. I handed Ethan and Todd my card.

Todd put out his hand again. "Hey, did you know that kid that drowned in the river?"

A guy rolled past pulling a cooler of canned beers on ice. He was wearing an empty 12-pack box of Bud as a hat.

"Which kid?"

Ethan pitched in. "He was crew. A P.A. Maybe?"

Todd looked around. I couldn't tell if he was genuinely pulled into the beauty and culture around us or if he was back to being aloof. "Yeah, we met him for a minute but we didn't go with him."

I guessed aloof. "Why not?"

"In a world of us and thems, he was always going to be a them."

Sadly, I knew just what he meant. "And he drowned in the Mississippi? Where? How? Why?"

Ethan laughed. "Slow down, Columbo. I'm sure it'll be on the news when you get home. There's a video."

"There's a video? Of a drowning? Color me intrigued. Is he dead? Did they find his body?"

Todd typed on his phone. The tattoo said, "FEAR" across one hand. I guessed the other said, "NO," but it was hard to be sure. He didn't lift his eyes as he spoke. "They're looking for him."

Tom looked over at me and I was done. "I gotta go. It was nice meeting you." I yelled over my shoulder, "Have fun in town. Let me know if you need anything." Tom seemed uncomfortable when I returned to his side. "I think I just got an audition."

He looked over at Ethan and Todd and put his hand on my hip. "From those guys? That's great. We'll stop on the way back for a celebration cocktail before we call it a day."

Afterward, I was a little disappointed Tom didn't want to come over. That said, I was going to need hours to go through all my photos for the blog and think of a way to describe something magical, laborious, profound and beyond words. It was probably for the best Tom didn't join me. I was glad we'd carpooled so I wouldn't worry about him driving.

Sofia's call came through just as I was downloading the cameras. She was laughing when I picked up. "I just posted something on your Facebook page."

I laughed. "I don't think that's how it's supposed to work. I don't think you're supposed to post something then call the person."

"I know, right? Don't tell anyone or they'll know we're old. But go look at it later. You'll laugh." She laughed some more. Clearly she was getting a real kick out of herself. My best friend since high school, Sofia knew me like a sister, or at least a close cousin. "So how was it, the Indians?"

"Amazing. Indescribable."

"That's inconvenient."

I laughed. "Yep. I'm hoping video and photos are worth a million words, but I'm not optimistic. It was just... a sensory overload." I watched the images flashing rapid fire as they loaded. "He drank a lot again today. He says it's to celebrate stuff I do but it's not really for me. I'd rather have a sno-ball. He's a fun drunk but he drinks a lot. Like, a lot. And often."

"But isn't that the thing down there? Drinking? Maybe you're just being sensitive because of your ex. I know it was like a million years ago before you even lived in L.A. but maybe you're just waiting for the other shoe to drop because the guys here were so..."

"I couldn't do another date in L.A. After the statue-of-the-dead-mother guy, I was done. Out. Cured of even wanting to try."

"You just gotta figure out if the drinking is a deal breaker."

"Good golly, I hope not. I've moved to a city people travel to for the express purpose of drinking too much."

"Yeah, but those are the tourists. You're always saying that. I'm just saying, compared to your dates out here, it's maybe not so bad."

"But he might be an alcoholic. Which would suck."

"But he's a happy drunk, right? There are worse things."

I laughed. "Maybe. Probably. Definitely. Dating out there was like a game of chicken. Everybody's just trying to figure out how far they can push you before you cry uncle."

"Right? Versus having fun and making memories. And learning stuff. You love learning stuff."

"It's true. I do. It's fine. It's just my history wanting to be heard. My cameras are done unloading. I'm dying for you to see this so I'm gonna go."

"Okay. Have fun. For real. Worry when an actual problem shows up."

I laughed again. "Good point. There's always one of those lurking around some corner."

"Right? So have fun until then. For real. Just try to relax into it a little and see what happens. Don't forget to look at Facebook." She hung up mid-laugh.

I opened a browser window and scrolled to Sofia's post, an adorable photo of her and little Nia

8

wearing the beads and other throws I'd sent after the parades. Nia clutched two of the stuffed animals I'd caught along with a sign that read, "Miss you!" The plastic tiara I hoped she'd love sat crookedly on her thin blonde hair. My finger tapped on the metal pad and the little arrow clicked "like."

I loaded the Indian shots into a slideshow, hit play and relived the creativity, industriousness, beauty, showmanship, commitment, culture and fun of the day. It was nearly impossible to narrow down my photo choices.

Every Sunday for over a decade, Sofia and I enjoyed what we dubbed, "Craft Sunday." It was no Super Sunday, but we would visit, listen to 70's music and craft – usually crochet, knitting or making elaborate ornaments for Christmas. Looking at the workmanship that went into the Indians' suits, I thought of my many Craft Sundays and the bond they created between Sofia and me. I thought about the beautiful things we made and the sense of accomplishment and whimsy the crafts gave us. Craft Sunday was the only thing I really missed about Los Angeles. Watching the super-masculine warrior men in bright plumage, I couldn't help picturing them hunched over a patch of fabric, painstakingly affixing bead after bead after bead after bead. It was sexy to me. The tedious dedication to making something unique and beautiful was something I could fully relate to, feel and understand. I liked thinking it was one of the things that made me good at acting.

I watched and edited the video then turned on the news and loaded all the media into my blog. The pretty and authoritative, "sophisticated" newscaster explained that authorities were searching for a twenty-three year old from Minnesota who they feared had drowned in the Mississippi. She said the guy had been drawn here by the allure of "Hollywood South." He'd found work on three movies as a P.A., a Production Assistant.

Then the video appeared, grainy and dark. I looked away, back to my computer screen. I wasn't fond of the information highway being so filled with snuff films disguised as right-to-know news. Unless it was about false allegations, I never saw the point and thought it robbed the family of some peace and a chance at closure.

The newscaster finished by saying the search was ongoing but hopes were growing dim. The screen filled with an image of the guy as we were urged to contact authorities if we had any information on his whereabouts.

He actually looked familiar. I rewound the broadcast to the spelling of his name. Keith Dalton. I looked him up in IMDbPro. Three movies. *Stealing Tomorrow* was the first movie I did here. His profile didn't have a photo so I fast-forwarded the TV to the one on the news. Yeah, I kinda remembered him. Maybe? He looked familiar. That was the truest thing I could say.

Chapter 2

I was thrilled to find my Super Sunday blog had twenty hits before I'd even shaken the sleep from my eyes. The post on my Facebook private page had lots of "likes." There were even a handful of likes on the public page, including a couple of new people who were now following my page. It felt good, like I was helping spread beauty.

It was Sofia who had forced me to finally give in and get on Facebook. I started the private page for friends and family and a public page for people who followed my acting and producing career. After blogging throughout the Saints historic run to their Super Bowl victory during Mardi Gras, I'd been discovered by a bunch of readers. Considering the anonymous little blog was only intended for Mom, Sofia and the friends I'd left behind in Los Angeles, I was pleased. Tom once told his friends to check it out and I got eighty-three hits in one day. Apparently, a few of them had shared the link on Facebook and it spread a little. Sofia was done hearing my resistance and fears after that.

Now, every time I wrote a blog post about my love for New Orleans, I shared it on both my pages. I had to admit it was working. Locals liked finding photos and videos of themselves having a great time. Tourists liked finding frontline information. But the best part was the people who'd left after The Storm and weren't able to come back. It helped them to be at parades and events vicariously. Those comments were my favorites. I kept all of the people and their comments and likes in mind when I took out my camera at events or sat at my computer to write. Though I was only averaging about thirty hits per post, somewhere out there, people who weren't Mom and Sofia were reading my words and enjoying the photos.

One of the new people following my public page also sent me a friend request so I clicked on their page. No photo, just an icon of a flexed muscle. No personal information and not many friends. Too little to base a "friendship" on. He'd reposted a few things, mostly about fitness, and the video everyone seemed to be sharing - the missing guy falling into the river.

The computer clicked softly as I closed it. The back door creaked open with a hard tug and I stuck my arm through to check the air outside. It was a great day for a walk, breezy and balmy. Jeans and no jacket weather. Soon enough, it would be skirt and tank top weather - my favorite.

Downstairs, I opened the front door and found a slip from the postman saying that he'd tried (and failed) to reach me about a package. Dang, I had to fix that damn doorbell. Now I was going to have to figure out picking up something that had been just feet from me while I was home.

It brought back all the frustration of living in a secured building in L.A. where the postal workers would just leave a slip in my box without even trying to contact me. I dropped the notification on the mantle inside and closed the door. Popping headphones in, I took a deep breath with my eyes closed. When I opened them, I was in my favorite city in the world and everything felt okay again.

The regal manor homes of the Garden District lit my imagination on fire. New Orleans was almost three hundred years old, decades older than America, and much of it was preserved. Sometimes I would try to imagine it was the 1800's or even the 1700's. I would try to un-see the cars, pavement and power lines and focus on hearing horse hooves and the jangle of reigns. Sometimes, I could picture everyone in costume. Even myself. I would try to imagine being my great-great-great-grandmother, Lily, my hoop skirt bobbing around me. Perhaps a parasol in one hand and a fan in the other. Maybe Lily's "other mother" still carried her parasol even though they'd made her a free woman.

It was nearly impossible to imagine the complicated relationship between Lily and her "other mother." Honestly, I hadn't figured out that Sassy was paid to raise my mother until I'd already been loving her as family for my entire childhood. By the time we buried Sassy last December, she'd also raised my cousins and their children as well as her own daughters. I was glad I had been able to assist Sassy's twins in tracking down their birth mother's identity. I hoped it helped them mourn Sassy without all those lingering questions about how she came to raise them. Taffy and Chiffon were very grateful and it felt so good to be of use to the grieving daughters.

Two guys rode a rusty, blue bike past me down Magazine. The wiry teenager sat on the front of the handlebars, his feet perched on the front axle, while the guy in his twenties peddled. Sweat formed at the cyclist's temples and the sun lit up droplets in his short afro like tiny diamonds sparkling in a crown. I smiled as they rolled past.

My walks here were flat. Los Angeles was full of hills. There were big views reaching out to the Pacific. But a lot of times, the higher you got, the easier it was to see the thick layer of orange smog we were living inside. The further I got from L.A., the thicker the fog that separated us.

Many of the homes in L.A. were pretty, but walls and gates often blocked the view as opposed to the inviting gardens that gave this neighborhood its name. Back in the day, the Europeans downtown thought the Americans uptown were tacky for planting gardens in front of their homes. The Americans apparently used the fragrant flowers to combat the scent of manure wafting from the road into their regal homes. The sweet olive trees were easily my favorite blooms. Their scent was thick like the abundant jasmine winding around wrought iron fences, but it had a citrus kick. It was probably one of the most wonderful scents in the world that didn't involve food.

Albert was standing outside the Sabai jewelry store as he often did. Long salt-and-pepper dreads covered his milky eye. He smiled when he spotted me and opened his arms. We hugged. He always smelled like Ivory soap. Though I thought of him as a man of the streets, he didn't seem to be homeless. I was certain he had a heck of a story. He gestured to the sky, the air and the world. "Look at this day! So pretty. Such a pretty, blessed day." Albert was the first friend I'd made in New Orleans without my cousins' involvement.

"It's beautiful." I noticed the front page of the paper through the scratched plastic window of a yellow dispenser behind Albert. The headline read, "Search Continues." A photo of the missing kid and a grainy shot from the video accompanied the article.

Albert followed my gaze. "Shame 'bout that boy. Come to the city full of dreams. Now be lucky to leave in a body bag."

I was surprised. Albert was usually so cheerful. "You don't think they'll find him?"

"They don't call it the Mighty Mississippi for nothin', no."

"Yeah but stranger things have happened. Heck, the Saints won the Super Bowl!"

A passerby interjected, "Who dat!" I loved this city.

It had started to rain when I got back to my block carrying groceries. The mail truck sat at the next corner. I thought of running to ask for my package so I wouldn't have to GPS my way to some post office. But it was raining, and I had groceries and just then the truck pulled away from the curb. I trudged toward the house as droplets streaked down my transitioning sunglasses. I started feeling that L.A. frustration again as one of the plastic grocery bags caught on the gate and I had to disentangle it without tearing the translucently-thin bag. "Come on! Are you kidding me?" As I gathered myself and the bags, the mail truck pulled up next to me.

The postman smiled from under his blue cap.

"Are you the resident here?"

"Yeah, in one of the units. Do you have a package for me? I'm in two."

"That's it. I came by earlier and left you a slip. You have it? I came by again 'cause I saw your car still settin' out front and figured maybe you were in the tub when I come by earlier. I thought that was you I saw when I was pullin' out. Circled back 'round on the chance."

I stared at him.

He lifted his eyebrows. "You got that slip?"

"Right. It's inside. Can you wait?"

"Happy to. You the one gettin' rained on."

My mind was racing as I hustled down the stone walkway. He knew my car? And what I looked like? And obviously where I live. That was the basis of our entire relationship. But he'd used all that information to specifically save me the trouble of tracking down my mail. Really?

I remembered the guy in my building who watched me change out a battery in my car. I was wearing a skirt and heels. He offered no help. Not even a nod of encouragement as he buffed his car three spaces away. He was the same guy I saw in the elevator the time I was carrying seven grocery bags and a twelve-pack of sodas. He stood there watching as I scrambled, trying to hit the button before the doors closed. He literally would have only had to lift a finger to help me and he just watched me struggle. He wasn't even evil about it, just indifferent.

I handed the postman the slip and he smiled as he gave me the package. I smiled back, wet strawberry-blonde curls stuck to my face. "Thank you so much for waiting and for coming back. That was very kind of you."

"Just doin' my day. Have a good one."

I looked at the return address. Sofia. The postman knew where I'd come from because of my forwarded mail. He saw all the names and addresses of my friends and family who'd sent cards or gifts to celebrate my move. He knew who paid me and who I owed. He might even have noticed the times I sent mail to Academy Award winner Clarence Pool, one of the most well known filmmakers of our time. So the postman would have access to Clarence's address too.

Every postperson I'd ever had would have had that information. But until this moment, none of them seemed to notice me. Part of me wanted to panic. Did all my neighbors know my car? Did they notice my comings and goings? I'd always teased that in L.A., only the smell would have alerted others to my demise. Here, people noticed each other.

In the era of identity theft, the whole thing gave me pause, but the overwhelming feeling I was having was that maybe I was becoming part of a community. It was like when Steve Martin's character in *The Jerk* discovered his name in the phone book and felt like a somebody. I felt like a neighbor in a neighborhood and it felt really good, like some kind of hug. But I couldn't stop thinking about how much trust we put in people who come by our house almost every day. And actually know who we are.

How many other things like that were different here? What other sudden intimacies would I find around the next corner? Tom still knew a bunch of his friends from high school. He worked with his cousin.

He stayed at his mom's a few times a month. He knew a lot about the people in his everyday life. Though I'd been in the industry long enough to work with some of the same people more than once, as an actor I hopped from set to set meeting literally hundreds of people each time. Even a commercial usually had a crew of at least fifty. If not for Sofia and the loyalty of Clarence, I would have felt far too alone, like a beachball lost in the ocean. The shark-filled and stormy ocean.

Sofia's package was full of goodies from Trader Joe's. I'd mentioned missing the chocolates and kettle corn in one of my blogs. I felt like the Julie character in *Julie and Julia* when her blog led to people sending food.

My mother used to be a therapist and said that movies were emotional shorthand. She said they allowed two unrelated people to communicate complex feelings by saying something like, "Did you see that scene in *What's Eating Gilbert Grape* where Johnny Depp leaves Leonardo DiCaprio in the tub and comes home and finds him still there shivering – it was like that." It felt legitimizing somehow for Mom to see that value in my work. And I felt glad knowing that movies helped people communicate and let others inside.

Maybe it was a good thing that my postman knew so much about me. Maybe it was a good thing to be on Facebook and allow people to connect with me - allow myself to connect with them. Reconnect, in many cases. But I was waiting for the other shoe to drop. The internet was at least as shark-infested as L.A. Rule number one for both - you never know who someone is until you know them. And even then, anything could happen.

The computer screen was already open to my blog stats so I clicked to refresh the page. Forty-seven hits! Maybe Tom would share it and really get the numbers going. Not that I would ask. There was far too much rejection built into my career for me to go looking for it in my relationships.

I looked around at my new place, a one-bedroom unit in the manor home my family built when they settled here after the Civil War. I loved the stained glass window in the bathroom and the super-high ceilings. I moved the boxes I hadn't found homes for into the hallway to remind myself to take them to Aunt Ava's next time I went across the lake. I wanted to be done with moving. I wanted it all in the rearview mirror of my life.

Driving the truck across country, I fully expected to cry when I crossed the California line. I'd worked hard to build a happy life and a good career out there. I was sure there were plenty of struggling actors who would have happily given up the happy-life part for the good-career part, but the more I worked, the harder it got to be happy. Especially when it came to men.

So as I drove over the state line and passed the sign telling me I was leaving California, I felt... relieved. Giddy even. I was forty-five and it had been nearly twenty years since the last time I packed up and left everything I knew behind, but this was different. I wasn't moving to some foreign world I'd only seen in movies. I was moving to the place I'd always thought should have been my home.

Moving to New Orleans had been like feeling adopted in every other city and finally finding my birth mother. Every time I returned to my family's hometown, I always felt like I understood why I was the way I was. I felt normal in this city's version of weird. Maybe it was ironic that, after attending a family funeral last December, tracking down a birth mother had kept me here long enough to decide to stay. When I finally went back to Los Angeles to pack up my things and say my goodbyes, I felt like a stranger in a strange land - but without all the wide-eyed hunger I had when I first arrived there so long ago.

Leaving L.A. after eighteen years had been easier than I thought it would be. My friends were sad to see me go, but they all seemed so excited for me. Not one of them brought up that I might be ending my career just as it was really taking off. When I forced the topic on Sofia, she was unshakable in her faith that I was going to work more than ever. Big fish, small pond - that was her basic argument.

I had to admit she wasn't wrong. I'd only been living here for about four months, the first two of which I'd spent on family business, Mardi Gras and the Saints winning season - and I'd already done two movies. It took me two years to get my first job in L.A.

I opened the plastic tub of dark chocolate covered almonds and popped two like vitamins.

Chapter 3

Easter started with rainbows dancing on the wall, shooting through the crystals of Sassy's chandelier. I decided to see them as a perfectly timed symbol of rebirth. L.A. hadn't always been gentle with me. Among the many reasons I decided to stay in New Orleans after Sassy's funeral was to start anew, experience a rebirth. I wanted to return to the girl I was before D.C., New York and L.A. took their toll, made me tough. I didn't want to be tough anymore. I wanted to be strong. It was beginning to sink in that I really lived here now, in my favorite city in the world. Every day, I felt a little better. More myself. Happier.

When I came to location scout for a movie last year, my business partner was downright disturbed by the locals and asked, "Why are the people here so… nice?" I answered that it was because they're happy. Being happy didn't seem to be a goal in Los Angeles. People moved there to pursue a dream, to find their fortune and/or fame, not to find love, make a home for themselves, be happy. Maybe I was just a dreamer for wanting to have my cake and eat it too. I'd gotten to do something I loved for a living for most of my adult life. Maybe that was supposed to be enough. But it wasn't. So, I was hoping that Easter would be a powerful rebirth for me. From career gal to happy woman. From tough to strong.

I chose a colorful and feminine dress that flowed out and rippled when I walked. Tom was spending the day with his family and I was joining mine in the heart of the French Quarter. My cousin May had a friend who was out of town and had offered up their home. It was kind of weird we weren't all eating dinner downstairs. Now the whole downstairs was rental unit one. I'd met the neighbor, and she seemed nice. Tom played kick ball with Jason next door to me in unit three.

The streetcar was pulling up just as I was hitting St. Charles. Running to meet it at the corner, my cheerful Easter dress flowed dramatically. I tried to catch my breath as I followed the short line to insert exact payment. I was still digging for the dollar-twenty-five when the last passenger paid. "I'm so sorry. I know I have it." My body was starting to shake a little.

The driver reached for a lever and pulled it, shutting the door behind me. "Relax baby, it'll all get done."

The streetcar lurched forward as I steadied myself and kept digging for the quarter. Was it that obvious? Did I seem uptight? Uncool?

I finally paid then searched for an empty seat on the crowded car. I couldn't help but notice the handsome tall guy standing in the back. Maybe it wouldn't be the worst thing if I didn't find a seat.

I scanned the rows looking for an opening. It was fairly normal to spot celebrities in L.A. If someone looked like Tom Cruise, it was probably Tom Cruise. Nevertheless, I was surprised to find Bryan Batt smiling at me. He nodded to the empty seat next to him. I had never actually seen an episode of *Mad Men*, but I knew he was supposed to be amazing on it as the closeted homosexual. Won awards. And I loved him in *Jeffrey*. Plus he was a theatre actor. I always felt a kinship with theatre-trained actors. The kid in the hoodie sitting behind him looked vaguely familiar but he looked toward the window as I approached, obscuring his face with the pale grey hood.

I smiled as I slid in next to Bryan on the wooden bench. "Thank you."

He tipped his barbershop-style straw hat at me. His smile was downright dazzling. "Of course. Happy Easter!"

"Yes! Happy Easter."

"Lovely day for it."

"Kinda perfect actually."

We both looked away for a moment. Silently. The bitterly cold winter had afforded us the rare treat of a true Spring with balmy temperatures and gentle breezes that pushed through the open windows. The massive live oaks overhanging the street were still littered with Mardi Gras beads in shiny colors. It was like the city was wearing jewelry.

"It's like the city's wearing jewelry."

I laughed. "Exactly." I liked this guy. Why were the good ones always gay? He was absurdly handsome. Chiseled cheekbones, a strong jaw, laughing eyes and that dynamite smile. Give me a break.

We chatted all the way to Canal Street and found we would be walking the same direction through the French Quarter. I caught the eye of the handsome tall guy as he made his way to the back exit. I smiled. He smiled back and my heart leapt a little. I used to love when that happened. It always meant I would end up dating that guy at some point. But I'd taken stock of this "sign" long ago - I may have dated the heart-leapers, but they were all ex's now. Tom was fun, and I was slowly letting myself fall for him. I was also assessing his faults and deciding whether I could live with them. It seemed a far more adult approach than following heart-leaps. That said, so far I had a zero percent success rate with all of my approaches.

Bryan extended his hand to help me down the stairs. "Well that almost couldn't have taken longer, but I think we can make it in time for the parade."

"There's an Easter Parade?"

He laughed as I followed him across Canal. "Oh honey, there are three today. We already missed one, but there's Chris Owens if we hurry and the Gay Parade later."

"Chris Owens from the club? The burlesque diva? Isn't she like seventy?"

"She wishes! But yes, the club owner." We were beginning to pass people wearing festive hats in dyed-egg colors. "Many of the riders are dancers and retired dancers. The bonnets are fabulous."

We caught up to the parade close to the start. The pot-holed streets were lined with locals and tourists. Many local men were wearing seersucker or linen suits with women in flirty sundresses or pastel monochromatic church ensembles. Everyone wore hats. I felt like I did on my first Saints game day when I came into the French Quarter and everyone but me was wearing black and gold. I was clearly going to have to start thinking more festively when dressing.

Bryan squeezed my hand. "You're about three blocks from your address. I'm going to try to find my family on the route. Would you like to come with?"

I often enjoyed meeting new people but it seemed like a natural break in our time together. "I think I'm going to stay put and film for my blog. I'll find my cousins after."

The sun literally glinted off his impossibly perfect thick, dark hair with greying sideburns. "It was a delight meeting you, Charlotte. May our paths cross again soon."

"Yes! And happy Easter." I hugged him.

"Yes, happy Easter."

I found a spot between a family wearing bunny ears and two women in pink wigs decorated with plastic eggs and silk flowers. Floats rolled by festooned with richly painted plaster bunting and flowers. Chris Owens looked like a Barbie - all legs, boobs and plastic. I wasn't used to seeing plastic surgery anymore, but she looked pretty amazing any way you sliced it. Especially if the rumors of her age hovering somewhere around eighty were true.

The riders in the floats that followed ranged from her peers to twenty-somethings. The bloom may have been off some of those roses, but they were all sexy, fun women and the crowd loved them. The men too. There was something very sexy about their whimsical abandon and willingness to be silly.

Bryan was right, the bonnets were fabulous. My favorite had a big, stuffed yellow chick sitting in a nest of silk daisies. I also loved the baby blue one covered in lavender silk flowers with a brim so large, it flopped over the rider's face like a collapsed umbrella.

A kid-sized train rolled past carrying people throwing candy followed by a man dancing alone. Our city was still after-glowing from the Saints' recent Super Bowl win so many of us joined in chanting "Who Dat!" along with the K. Gates redux of the Ying Yang Twins' *Halftime (Stand Up and Get Crunk)* pumping from the party-bus behind the dancing man. Wearing an oversized, white undershirt and jeans, he was obviously a local who'd jumped into the procession. He tossed his baseball cap in the air, spun and caught it behind himself. The wig ladies and I were loving it but the party-bus driver was getting agitated at being slowed down to accommodate hat tricks. I jumped when the bus honked. People around here usually saved honking for celebrations. The dancing man pulled his cap down over his short 'fro then jumped out of the way.

After the police car finished the parade, I made my way down Royal Street toward May's friends' house. The clarinet lady and her family were playing in front of the Rouses Market. A couple in white finery topped with straw hats danced and twirled as two women swayed and tried to figure out who should lead. There was nothing like this in L.A. Except movie sets. Movie sets could be magical at times.

Aunt Ava was standing in front of the house with four drag queens in sequin gowns as I walked up. With their high hair and Easter adornments, the queens all towered over Ava. She was clearly holding court and had them all laughing. May came out of the front door carrying four plastic go-cups of some yellow beverage on ice. "There she is! Charlotte, take a picture."

I pulled out my camera and snapped a shot of her on the porch. May posed dramatically after I snapped and I grabbed one more shot. She laughed, "I meant of Mama and her friends."

Aunt Ava struck a supermodel pose with the other queens and I took a few shots. May passed out drinks as I made my way through the post-Katrina-remodeled house. It was kind of odd to see these more modern interiors inside centuries-old homes. My cousins were in the courtyard out back. Lillibette handed me a fat, pink sidewalk chalk. I looked down and saw they'd been drawing shapes in different colors. Lillibette turned to the group. "Charlotte can draw it." She looked at me with her blue eyes - the kind with a navy rim and icy, pale blue inside. "Charlotte, draw us a butterfly."

May handed me the bucket of chalks, and Tate took funny glasses off and put them on my face. "Look at the drawings."

I was beginning to wonder how much they'd had to drink already. Then I saw it - the shapes were 3D. I lifted the glasses. Plain old chalk drawings. I lowered the glasses. 3D shapes jumping off the concrete. I was in. I put all the supplies down and started on the butterfly, arranging my skirt around me. "Do y'all watch *Mad Men*?"

No one had. Tate didn't even turn on his TV unless the Saints were playing. He'd never seen me in a movie either. He spent his spare time fishing. I almost envied his ability to sit and watch a lake do nothing for hours.

May and her husband thought they had seen the show, but they were confusing it with some other program. Lillibette had heard of it.

Aunt Ava came to the back door. "I need someone to carry the ham to the buffet."

May peered at my handiwork through the glasses. "Go Charlotte!"

Lillibette looked up to Ava standing in the doorway, leaning her weight on perfectly manicured nails. "Mama, did you say you watch that Mad Men show?"

Ava fixed the chain tassel dangling from her necklace pendant. "Yes, that's the one with the Batt boy in it, the Pontchartrain Beach boy. His parents owned the amusement park, remember?"

I ventured, "Bryan Batt? That's who I met on the streetcar. That's what I was going to tell you. Nice guy. Offered me a seat like a true gentleman then walked me to the parade."

Tate laughed. "I always wanted to be that kid. He pretty much grew up in Disneyland. I used to dream about it."

We all daydreamed with Tate about riding rides and eating cotton candy as everyone took turns looking at my 3D butterfly.

I was so glad to be surrounded by family. It made me feel strong and not even a little tough.

Chapter 4

It was another beautiful day for a walk. I put on my headphones and listened to a shuffle of hip hop and 70's songs. *Jungle Boogie* ended as I turned on St. Charles and Eminem began rapping. Beads dangled from the live oaks, and I could almost see the floats slowly rolling between dance troupes and school bands. I wished I was listening to *Mardi Gras Mambo* or *Carnival Time*. My music seemed suddenly angry. I clicked forward five or six times then landed on the Allman Brothers' *Midnight Rider*. Good enough.

The line in the post office was long. A sign instructed that no one on a cell phone would be served. I wasn't sure I'd grabbed the right forms but I filled them out anyway. A teenaged boy balanced his boxes on one hand. Some neighbors laughed realizing they could've driven together. Two women in their sixties discussed the upcoming Saints draft. The line was taking forever. The employees were probably getting hungry and irritable. I hoped I had the right forms.

The guy in the Hornets jersey tapped my hand. "They callin' you."

I snapped to attention. "Sorry! Thanks. So sorry."

He smiled gently. "Just lettin' you know."

Of course I didn't have the right forms. I started to

get anxious. The place was closing, the line was still so long and I didn't want anyone "going postal" on me. "Just get the forms from over there?" I pointed to the display on the other side of the room, past all the people waiting. The earth-mother in a blue uniform nodded wordlessly. I worried I was frustrating her. "Can I leave my stuff here? No, never mind. You've got enough to do. I'll just take it with me."

The earth-mother postal worker smiled and laughed a little. Her voice was buttery. "Relax baby, it'll all get done. Leave your stuff if you feel and just bring them forms back when you ready."

I felt suddenly ridiculous. Even busy postal workers were more relaxed than I was. I was uptight. I was so uptight that it was obvious to multiple strangers. People always said L.A. was so "laid back." Maybe laid back didn't mean relaxed there. Maybe it meant detached. Whatever it meant, it was downright neurotic compared to a busy post office in New Orleans.

I tried focusing on my breathing on the walk home. I wanted to work hard at relaxing but even with my stubborn brain, I understood that wasn't how relaxation worked. I breathed in my nose to the count of eight and out my mouth to the count of eight. In. Out. In. Out.

I kept breathing all the way up the stairs and even as I found my keys and turned the lock. I could hear my phone ringing and rushed to grab it before the machine caught the call. Tom's now-familiar voice greeted me. "Hey Slim. You just getting in? You sound outa breath."

"Yeah, I was at the door when I heard the ringing.

You stuck at work?"

"Knee deep in wetlands. It's pretty bad. The erosion. Katrina didn't teach people a damn thing."

I fell back onto the bed and stared up at Sassy's chandelier. "We forget. It's an old saying. It means history is doomed to repeat itself."

"Doomed. That's about the size of it. Listen, I'm gonna hang with the guys tonight. Go hang at Boudoux's. I'm officially down and it's still early in our time for you to be seein' me depressed. We'll have a good day at the French Quarter Fest. You'll love it."

"I don't only have to see you at your best." Why did I always do that? I liked having fun with him. Maybe he was wise to keep things fun as long as possible.

Tom laughed. "Steady, Slim. Get out while you still can. I'll see you soon."

"Bye." I hung up and looked to the chandelier as I walked out of the bedroom and down the long hallway. I had paintings hung now. Photos on shelves. I was home.

Commercials were running as the TV popped to life. One for Mo' Money Taxes. A limo rolled up and three guys stepped out wearing sharp suits and a fair bit of bling. Their ensembles didn't exactly scream, "taxes."

Then one for Cox cable service. People said "Cox" around here all the time and never seemed to hear themselves. I wasn't really the sort to go in for *Beavis and Butthead* humor, but the good people of Cox Communications were pushing the limit of my decorum. This commercial was promising, "Cox Business – a better fit. Keep your business fit – with

Cox." I couldn't help hearing Tina Fey sleazy-whispering in my ear, "Your lady business."

My favorite tagline so far was, "No one's working faster than Cox." Faster, Cox, faster! During Carnival, a Cox truck opened many of the parades and the children would yell, "Cox! Cox!" No one seemed to notice. I'd been laughing at these commercials since moving here, but everyone around me was just getting information on the new low price of "Cox bundling."

Culture was a funny thing. Things like "normal" and "laughable" were a matter of perspective. It was liberating and unnerving to see Los Angeles from this distance. Mostly it was funny to be the insider looking out, but every once in a while, it was a Beavis-and-Butthead chuckle-fest to be the outsider looking in.

The next commercial was also for Cox. "Powerboost – It's an extra burst of speed when you need it most that you can only get with Cox." Blue graphics filled a white screen. "Powerboost from Cox is smart enough to recognize large upload and download demands automatically." They had to be doing this on purpose. Or maybe I needed to have my brain washed out with soap. Great, L.A. had made me an uptight perv.

The last spot was for the local news. French Quarter Fest announcements, a shooting then the photo of the missing kid. "Authorities are still searching for the body of a member of the Hollywood South community. Details at ten."

They'd started saying "body." Missing, presumed dead at this point I was guessing. I pushed a pile of notes from my laptop and sat at the blonde pine desk I'd bought with money from guest starring on *Seinfeld* in the 90's.

The Mardi Gras Indians photos were popular. I hadn't posted anything in days but the blog was getting dozens of hits. I'm not sure why I Googled the missing kid. I didn't really know him. His Facebook page was still active. Mostly people posting updates and links to news. I had mixed feelings about keeping people's pages open after death. It was a great place to exchange information and memorialize someone. But I never knew what to do when their birthday would pop up. And I always wondered who was clicking the "likes" for these dead people. Sometimes the dead person would even comment. It was a lot to process.

Someone posted wondering if everyone should put together a second line parade in memoriam. So far, only two people had liked it. Either Keith Dalton wasn't wildly popular or it seemed too soon to memorialize him.

His photos were mostly memes about working in the industry. There was the photo they'd been using in the news and a selfie of Keith at the base camp of a set. There were rows of white trailers behind him. A woman in a navy robe sat on trailer steps reading something. Probably her script. Wait. That was my wavy strawberry-blonde hair. Those were my long legs. That was me. I dragged the photo onto my desktop then scrolled to another. It was of a longish table with a bunch of people eating. Some were in costume. Two men were wearing the same exact suit, down to the yellow pocket square. An actor and his stunt double I guessed. I zoomed in. Bryan Batt and a Clark-Kent-looking, younger double. Small world.

There was only one other personal photo. A teenaged Keith Dalton on a dirt bike. I copied those photos onto the desktop as well, made a "missing kid" folder, dragged the photos into it and moved the file to the "etc." folder.

Wind rustled the hundreds-year-old live oak on the lot next door. Then the waxy leaves of the towering magnolia tree beside the house scratched and banged at the window screens above the desk. This had been my mother's room when she was growing up and her mother's childhood room before that. I liked thinking of Mama Heck rocking my Maw Maw beside these windows, then her daughter, Sassy, rocking my own mother beside these windows. How tall was the magnolia back then?

Sassy probably knew what that symbol on the chandelier meant. Mama Heck, too. One of them put that masking tape over the symbol and the initials. Right? Masking tape couldn't be more than a hundred years old. Were they hiding the etchings? Maybe that was why they were so adamant about making sure the chandelier was always hanging, always screwed into a ceiling with the etchings covered. That could be something. I wrote a note to myself and put it on the pile on my desk.

And why would Dad have the same symbol on his pipe? Maybe it was a gift from someone on Mom's side of the family. That could explain it easily enough. My fingers searched through the pile, pulling out a pencil drawing of the symbol. Why the symbol on the flask in May Baily's Place's brothel curio collection? Had the flask belonged to Maw Maw's father? It was strange trying to picture Paw Paw Perry at a brothel. He passed when I was seven, but I had a very clear impression of him as a gentle soul who positively doted on his wife and never even flirted after she passed.

But I didn't really know him. Maybe he was secretly an avid fan of prostitutes. There was an old Jewish saying that whenever a person dies, a library is burned. I wished I'd gotten to wander my family's libraries before they passed. At the very least, I wanted to know what that strange symbol was and why it seemed to be popping up everywhere.

Chapter 5

According to Tom, all of the parading, eating and drinking the city had been doing since I got here was all just a prelude to the dozens and dozens of annual festivals the city hosted. Unlike Jazz Fest, the food and music at French Quarter Fest were entirely local.

My new agent, Claudia, a rusty-voiced pro, had called with a last minute audition so I missed most of the day. Tom sat on a blanket with a few of his friends. Other friends were dancing on the flat ground closer to the stage. Nancy's tie-dye skirt filled with air as she spun and swayed. A warrior of a man with long, thick dreads danced in his own world on the other side of the grounds. Tom pointed to the tall, joyful woman singing onstage. "That's Margie Perez. She's one of us."

Tom's friends were a clique, like back in school. Except none of them dressed alike. Being a tall, thin "orange-haired" girl in school, I hadn't really had a clique until L.A. There was a two year period where I knew exactly what I was doing every weekend because we'd all get together at T.K.'s Malibu house, hang out by the pool and watch movies. I had to admit it was kinda cool. It wasn't all that different from eating crawfish and listening to music at Boudoux's house in the Treme. Except the L.A. clique included Oscar winners, some of *People*

Magazine's most beautiful people and a Kennedy or two. And people waited on us while we lounged around and found ways to keep each other amused. And a rotating crop of women came through digging for gold, or at least a good time and a story to brag. I liked knowing all the names of the women in Tom's clique, seeing the same faces every time. And they dressed to delight themselves more than to show off body parts for the guys.

A woman wearing a silk-flower-covered costume-dress roamed on and off the riverfront stage, dancing with her flower-covered parasol. I wasn't sure if she was part of the crowd or part of the show. As always, there were children and elderly mixed into the audience. That was how my family had always partied - all generations together. There were very few older people in L.A. And most of them didn't seem to be related to anyone. I used to joke that the city was like *Chitty Chitty Bang Bang* where the children were locked away together indoors.

The weather was perfect, and I focused on feeling the breeze coming off the river and over my skin. Tom was bopping his head to the music. He looked over to me and smiled. "Great, huh?"

I went to answer but he was already looking back to the band. A giant cruise ship passed downriver behind the stage. People on the decks waved to our crowd, some of whom waved back. I took a deep breath and let myself relax into the perfection of sitting on grass on a sunny day surrounded by new friends and total strangers all agreeing that we loved experiencing live music while people danced with abandon and ate delicious local food.

We cheered Margie on as she took a bow with her group. Still singing bits of the last song, we gathered our things and headed backstage. With bright yellow fabric neatly swirled atop her head, Margie appeared far taller than my five feet and ten inches. It was easy to find compliments as we were introduced. I dug the band's Afro-Caribbean rhythms and the high-energy show they gave. Margie's band had another gig so she couldn't join us as we headed to the show starting on a nearby stage. I began to wonder if she was the one in the clique who had a ridiculous schedule and had trouble getting together. I'd walked a mile in those shoes.

I felt my phone buzzing. Claudia. "Do you have a pen? I have good news."

"Go ahead." I pulled a pen from my shoulder bag and held it above my palm. "You just got a movie you didn't even audition for."

"I did? What movie? What's the part?"

Her voice was gravelly and soothing all at once. "It's a pool-cocktail party scene in a low budget heist movie. The director's Todd Brandt and the producer is Ethan---"

"Jacobs?"

"Yes. You know him?"

"Yeah, I just ran into them the other day. Super Sunday. Met the director."

"Well, I guess you left a good impression. They want you next week."

Following Tom and his friends to the next stage, I scribbled the details on my hand. Claudia promised an email would be waiting for me. I tried not to worry about the dates conflicting with Mom's upcoming visit. Especially because my niece, Julia, would be joining for her first visit since she was a toddler. I suddenly remembered my exciting invite. As the gang settled onto a patch of lawn, I grabbed Tom's hand. "I almost forgot!"

He spun me around and pulled my back to his chest. "Look. Uncle Lionel and his women." Tom had shown me this man with the Don Knotts body and the Isaac Hayes swagger the night we finally exchanged names. "Remember we saw him that night I ran into you at Krewe du Vieux? After the parade, someone stole his drum. Remember we saw him that night?"

"That's terrible. Someone stole his drum?"

"People freaked out. There were articles calling whoever did it ignorant or cruel. He made the drum himself. They say he clung to it for float during The Storm."

"That's crazy. Did he get it back?"

"Yeah, you right. It just showed back up one day. Never did find out who took it but shame brought it back. Shame and fear."

"That's an amazing story." I remembered again. "Oh, so I have a kinda cool invite. My friend, Carter, is having a movie premiere at the Prytania and he's invited me, my mom and my niece to come. You want to go? It'll be fun. Red carpet and everything. You can see a little of my world."

"What's the movie?"

I wasn't sure why it would matter. "*Contenders*. The sequel to *Contender*." I wasn't sure if Tom meant to jerk his hand away.

"Your friend is Carter Ellis?"

I felt suddenly self conscious. Carter was a global

movie star with an Oscar to boot. But I'd known him too long and too well to only see him that way. Sure, Carter Ellis was a huge star, but Carter was my warm, loyal, funny friend. "Yeah."

He snorted a laugh. "Of course. Of course that's your friend. I hated *Contender*."

"Oh." I wasn't sure what to say. It wasn't the response I expected. "Well, it still might be fun. Think about it and let me know if you want to go. It's the twenty-first so give me enough notice if I need to find another plus-one."

"Plus one?"

"Yeah, that's what they call it when you get to bring a guest."

"There are invitations that don't let you bring a guest?"

I could see I'd offended his upbringing. My brain searched for logic. It was the first time I'd questioned this practice in a long time. "Would an invite to a bachelor party let you bring a guest?"

"Depends. But is that what you meant? That there are bachelor party premieres that don't let you bring a guest?"

Of course not. "Sometimes, invites are really hard to come by and you can only bring yourself. It's kinda nice when you get a plus-one and I'm getting to bring my whole family so this is like a real friend of mine. Like you have real friends who invite you to come see them in concert." As if on cue, the next band, 101 Runners, filled the stage. I was thrilled to find they were dressed in their Mardi Gras Indian suits. Big Chief Monk Boudreaux walked to the center mic carrying a tambourine. He smacked the tambourine, shook it and cried out an Indian chant then smacked the tambourine skin again. The band sang out, "Indian Red." It was probably my favorite Mardi Gras Indian song. People sang along and I wished I knew the words. Of course I could learn them, but I wished I knew them - that I'd grown up singing this song and *Pocky Way*, *Mardi Gras Mambo* and so many more. And though Tom seemed to really enjoy teaching me everything about the city, sometimes I thought he wished I'd been born here too.

After the show, we gathered our things again and pushed into the standing-room-only crowd for Soul Rebels. We danced ourselves into a sweat as the raucous brass band played a mix of local standards, pop covers and originals. At some point, the band yelled out to the crowd, "Hello, New Orleans!" and I realized – they were talking to me. I was New Orleans. I was a transplant, but my new home had been built by my family after the Civil War. The horse buried in the back yard had pulled my family and their possessions from Texas. I was rooted here.

We finished the evening at Harry's Corner Bar in the Quarter. Tom seemed warmer as he got a little drunk. Boudoux wandered over swigging a Pabst Blue Ribbon as the jukebox played The Meters. "Tom, you realize she's out of your league, right?"

Tom clinked bottles with him. "Yeah, you right. Aim high!" I laughed but this was a bit familiar, this joking about me being too good to be in a real relationship with some mere mortal.

Boudoux smiled at me drunkenly. "When you come to your senses, remember that I can cook."

Tom pushed him playfully.

Boudoux lowered his head. "Fine, I'm no step up."

Lisa interjected, "You own your own home."

Boudoux smiled. "Yeah, you right. What about that?"

Tom threw a peanut at her. "Hush up, Lisa! Charlotte's no gold digger."

Lisa laughed, "True dat, or she'da skipped right over you." Everyone laughed. I wasn't sure how to feel.

Tom was sloppy-sweet walking back toward Boudoux's place. He stopped next to my car and leaned against the low trunk. "Are you good to drive?"

"Oh, I thought I was... Oh, you're crashing here tonight? I thought you were... Never mind. I want to sound cooler than this."

Tom laughed big. "Relax, Slim. We're good. I'm past being of any use tonight." He gave me a loose-lipped kiss. "I'll just see you Sunday."

"Sunday? I thought we were going to the Fest again tomorrow."

"I know. I promised my mother I'd help her move some things out of the attic. I'll probably just end up spending the day there."

"Okay. No, I get it. It's fine. I'll see you Sunday."

"You're allowed to be disappointed. You don't have to pretend it's fine. I said we'd go together and I'm standing you up."

I immediately felt better. "Yeah, kinda."

He kissed me again and I got into the car. He waved, "See you Sunday."

That would have to do.

Chapter 6

Lillibette handed me the program for the festival and payed the woman for the turtle and sherry soup from the Court of Two Sisters booth in Jackson Square. I took a taste of the flavorful brown brew and tried not to picture turtles. I enjoyed a few more spoonfuls then handed the bowl to Lillibette. She moaned a bit, "So good. Everybody says Commander's but I love Two Sisters." Lillibette pointed with her elbow, "Muriel's. We gotta hit that early or it'll never happen."

We took turns with the bowl of soup as we waited in what was by far the longest line in the Square. The older gentleman in front of us turned and asked if the soup was any good and where we'd gotten it. He was wearing a Saints jersey with signatures all over it and a Saints cap pulled over his yellowing eyes. Lillibette pointed back to the Two Sisters booth and he lifted his finger to match hers, "There?" His ashy hand was scarred with tiny cuts and I wondered if he was a Mardi Gras Indian. Maybe he was even a Big Chief. Anyone could turn out to be anyone here.

Lillibette pointed again and he nodded, "Yeah, I see where it's at. I'll have to go by there. I know y'all here for that crepe. Line long as hell but we here early enough. Not so bad this time a day."

I loved how easy it was to have a nice day here. I

loved being able to meet lots of people for no particular reason other than it felt good.

Half an hour later, Lillibette and I split the shrimp eggplant dressing and a well-worth-the-wait goat cheese crepe smothered in tenderly cooked crawfish in some fabulous kind of tomato cream sauce. The line for the chocolate hazelnut crepe with fresh sliced strawberries from Crepes a la Cart was only four people long, but they made each crepe to order so it took awhile.

I realized we'd been at the festival for hours and hadn't gone to see music. I'd clearly missed some of the best the fest had to offer when I was with Tom. There were a couple of stages in Jackson Square but it was the food that had our attention.

As if on cue, Lillibette asked for the program and unfolded it on the lawn. She ran her finger down the variously-colored schedule cubes. "Look! Anders Osborne is about to start. We gotta go!" She folded the schedule as I finished the last of the decadent crepe and wiped chocolate from my lips and fingers.

We'd seen Anders Osborne at a free concert at Tipitina's when I came for Sassy's funeral. When he sang *Louisiana Rain*, it was like a call to something deep in my soul saying, "Stop feeling like a stranger in strange lands and COME HOME." I liked that his originals were becoming familiar to me. I sang along to parts of *On the Road to Charlie Parker* and *Love is Taking its Toll*. We danced and swayed for over an hour. As the sky over the river was turning golden with sunset, Osborne dove into *Louisiana Rain*. My eyes welled with happy-tears. I realized in a shot that I would die on this dirt. I'd had a big adventure, seen lots of things, met lots of people and visited many places, but I could be happy here just eating and listening to music.

It wasn't until the break between bands that Lillibette finally asked, "What happened to Tom? Work?"

"Naw, his mom needed help with stuff in the attic or something. I'll see him tomorrow."

"Too bad he missed today. Especially him spending the day in and out of an attic."

I suddenly felt bad. "I hadn't really thought about that. I was too busy thinking it sucked for me and wondering if it means something that he'd rather do that than this."

"Damn. Well at least you know you're selfish."

"I prefer self-centered. It sounds more balanced, like something I worked for."

Lillibette laughed. "If it makes you feel better."

The next band, Bonerama, featured three trombone players who could make their horns sound like guitars. It was wild to hear them take on *Whipping Post* and a few Zeppelin tunes. I was seventeen again, swinging my hair and hips wildly. I hated for it to end. Except the next band was local favorite Rebirth Brass Band - the stage's closer.

The crowd thickened to a fairly tight standing-room-only as the crew scrambled to reset the stage. Lillibette considered getting one last cocktail but reconsidered when she realized how many people filled the park alongside the river. There had to be thousands. And they all went bananas as the band took the stage. At least half the crowd seemed to know every song. I immediately recognized *Do*

Watcha Wanna. Back in L.A., I had a few stress relievers for when the city, my career, dating, all of it was getting to me. One of my favorite reliefs was a YouTube video of Rebirth second lining down Royal Street the day Jazz Fest began. It was clear they had no permits. There were no police escorts and at some point, the whole procession ran into a dead end and had to turn back on itself. I danced myself silly and happy-cried realizing this was no video. This was my life.

Lillibette was dancing with a man in a Saints jersey... covered in signatures. He yelled into her ear. She gave him a thumbs-up then yelled to me, "He got the turtle soup. He liked it."

Perfect.

When the show ended, we walked back into the Quarter with our turtle soup friend. "I'ma split off on Chartres. Got work tomorrow."

Lillibette's voice was filled with compassion. "On a Sunday? Oughta be a law. Even God rested on the seventh day."

"What do you do?"

Turtle soup man looked genuinely wounded at my question. I wasn't sure what I'd done wrong but I felt suddenly terrible, like I'd driven a wedge between us. He kept his eyes forward. "Maintenance."

Lillibette jumped in, "Charlotte just moved home. She's an actor."

"Yeah?" He looked genuinely curious. "You do plays?"

"No, movies and TV. Gotta pay my bills."

"I heard that. Y'all have a good night. Get home safe."

We waved as he headed down Chartres. Lillibette led the way to the car. It was cooler now that I wasn't dancing so I untied the sweater from my waist and threw it on. "It's so funny here. Everyone asks if I'm in theatre when they find out I'm an actor. In L.A., first of all, it's like a given that pretty much everyone's in the industry and the next logical question is like, 'Who's your agent?' or 'Have I seen you in anything?' And that's only if they take you seriously enough not to hit you with, "Oh yeah? Which restaurant?" There, actor mostly equalled waiter. Do people here make enough money to live doing theatre?"

"I don't think he was trying to figure out how much money you make."

"Wait, is that what I did? When I asked what he did for a living?"

"Not in so many words, but didn't you?"

I thought about that, about how I was drawing some line dividing us. We'd enjoyed many of the same things all day. We'd eaten and danced together. And I had pointed out a thing that might make us different. It honestly never occurred to me before that it might be rude to ask what people do for money. Now it seemed impossible not to see it as I replayed turtle soup man's reaction. For nearly two decades, "What do you do?" had been a standard question for most of my conversations. Heck, I usually asked within a few minutes and many used it as an opener with me. I was going to have to learn a whole new way to talk.

The missing kid was on the TV again when I got home. Officially presumed dead. Before I could unsee it, the video clip of him falling in the river played. They only showed him tripping and falling, then cut before he went under. Something about it bothered me. I rewound it and played the clip again. Just some kid falling in a river. Nothing special.

I loaded my camera into the laptop and started a slideshow to review the photos for the blog. The images flashed past in fast forward.

Who had shot the video of the kid? It was kind of a random thing to catch. Why would someone be filming the river at night? What could they have been attracted to? A passing boat? The lights on the bridge? I shook it off. Nowadays, who knew - maybe it was just a selfie gone bad, a horrifying photo-bomb. I changed the channel to *Law and Order* and went to work editing photos of another amazing day.

Chapter 7

I met Tom and the rest of the gang at Boudoux's house expecting we'd head over for the last day of the fest. The stereo blared a funky brass band as I passed through the empty living room and kitchen. Everyone was out back on the patio untying bags of live crawfish, potatoes, garlic bulbs, lemon wedges and corn cobs and dumping them into a giant metal basket. Tom and Boudoux lifted the cornucopia up and lowered it slowly into a gas-fired cauldron of boiling spiced water.

Lisa slap-wiped her hands on her red and black poodle skirt, rustling the red crinoline beneath. "They're small this year, even for this early."

Boudoux dumped more spice into the water. "Weather was too cold. Got over a hundred pounds. Should be plenty."

Tom held a live crawfish to his earlobe and attached it like an earring. The crawfish dangled. He grabbed another and held it to the other lobe. "Ouch!" He jumped sending both crawfish flying. One landed near Lisa's feet and she stooped to retrieve it. The other landed on John's lap as he was settling onto the stoop with a beer. He jumped up flipping the poor mudbug and throwing him in the direction of Nancy.

Tom slapped John on the arm. Hard.

"What?"

"Jerk! You threw it right at a girl."

"Manly man." Boudoux made a muscle.

John lowered himself slowly back onto the stoop like he feared he might have to jump up again. "What? That thing has claws. It landed right near my buddies. I can't have that. I need all this." He waved his hand over his lap like Vanna White presenting a prize.

Boudoux grabbed the crawfish from Lisa and tossed it at him. "Nobody waitin' on your buddies to start a party."

John looked genuinely angry as he jumped up again letting the crawfish miss him. Tom moved between them then finally spotted me. "Charlotte! Hey Slim." He walked over and hugged me just as John grabbed the garden hose and sprayed Boudoux who grabbed a damp hand-towel stained with cayenne and threw it uselessly.

I kept my eyes on the boiling pot of water as the patio became a water fight. I couldn't help being the cautious one. "Y'all should watch out for that boilin' pot. It's all fun and games 'til someone goes to the emergency room with third degree burns."

That was enough to stop all but John and Boudoux who'd apparently been fighting like puppies nipping at each other since they met in first grade.

Tom hustled me into the kitchen and snuck a kiss. "You had fun yesterday?"

"Yeah, you would've loved it. Anders, Rebirth, it was awesome. How's your mom?"

"She's herself but the attic is done. She had a whole honey-do list worked out. Guess Dad's not much help lately. Mom says he's been workin' a lot."

"Well, it's good you got that done." I hoped he'd mention missing me.

"Yeah, I actually made it to Rebirth. Caught the last half."

Really? "You shoulda called me."

"In that noise? You'da never heard it."

I laughed. "True dat. But I coulda met you after."

He fed me a cracker covered in cream cheese and pepper jelly. "I'm so glad you're here. The crawfish are small this year but there's plenty of 'em."

"I heard."

"Later we're watching that new show, *Treme*."

"In the Treme!"

"Yeah, you right." He fed me another cracker and nudged me toward the door. "Come on, those idiots are probably done killin' each other by now."

I wasn't sure how I felt about him calling his friends idiots.

The women grabbed a stack of newspapers as the men moved a long picnic table to the center of the brick patio. Everyone spread sections of the paper out across the wooden slats. I saw no chairs. John stood next to the middle of the table. "This is my spot. I'm claiming this." People filed in as Tom and Boudoux lifted the giant basket from the water and dumped it down the center of the table. Steam billowed from the pile. Tom joined me at the table as Boudoux lowered another sack-load of crawfish into the pot.

We pinched, picked and "sucked heads" through at least eighty pounds before finally stalling out. The sun began to set as a few people joined Boudoux inside to pick meat from tails for a gumbo. Nancy worked like a pro, filling her cereal bowl over and over. I was better at crabs and shrimp than crawfish so I lounged on a barstool and nibbled at leftover pork cracklins and boudin balls. I liked the mildly mushy texture of the balls of sausage made with rice. Boudoux had prepared the mixture and stuffed the casings himself. So many people here really knew how to cook. And plenty of people here caught or hunted their own food. Looking around the room at the mostly scruffy-faced beer-bellied men working away in the kitchen, I didn't miss the perfectly plucked, shaved and competitively-clothed men of L.A.

Everyone washed their hands with lemons and headed out to the patio - now totally reimagined as a movie theatre. Twinkle lights climbed the trunk of the magnolia. A sheet hung from the tall, slatted-wood fence. People lounged on blankets and pillows as the guy with the blonde hair whose name I never got fooled with a projector. Tom and I settled with our backs against the stoop and passed bowls of spiced popcorn.

From the opening shot, everyone had thoughts and opinions. New Orleanians could be highly protective of how their culture was portrayed. You almost had to feel badly for anyone who attempted to please them. But Nancy liked that they'd used the mold on the walls as the backdrop for the opening credits. And everyone agreed longtime-local John Goodman's activist-with-an-uncensored-mouth was perfect casting.

At some point, the camera passed right in front of Boudoux's house and we all went wild. I was used to being in places I'd seen in movies when I lived in

L.A., but this seemed somehow more meaningful. And the moment felt more alive because it was a shot of the house where we were all sitting - while we were watching the house onscreen. That had only happened to me once before when I watched *I love You, Man* at The Grove and they showed the movie theatre at The Grove onscreen.

Everyone seemed very worried that the violinist and her druggie boyfriend in the show were going to turn out to be the horrible post-Katrina story of the man who killed his girlfriend, chopped her up and cooked her then threw himself from the roof of the Omni hotel. No one wanted to watch that story. I guessed the character was based on the violinist I'd seen play outside Cafe du Monde but I didn't say anything. I figured they knew better than I did.

The Big Chief story-line had mixed reactions but we were all stunned into silence, peppered with the occasional "wow," when he donned his beautiful Mardi Gras Indian suit.

There was no debate when local legend Kermit Ruffins showed up and played at Vaughn's. He was a real crowd pleaser in the show and on our patio. Elvis Costello came up to Kermit when he was cooking on a barrel-grill outside the leaning, dilapidated bar. Costello asked him why he didn't want to go on the road, get famous, make money. Kermit swept his arm over the rusty barrel-grill, past drunken revelers and walls in need of paint and said in all seriousness, "And leave all this?" Exactly. It reminded me of a favorite local quote from the 1800's. Something about, "Times are not good here. The city is crumbling into ashes." Then details I forgot, then,

"But it is better to live here in sackcloth and ashes than to own the whole state of Ohio."

How would I have survived watching this show on my couch in L.A.? This show would have called me home even if Sassy's funeral hadn't. Every once in awhile, my industry would create something that made me proud to be a part of film and TV. As the show ended, the locals felt fairly well represented and like there was accuracy to the food, music, colloquialisms and much of the culture. They were even generous with their assessments of the actors' accents. I felt like my industry had successfully captured a snapshot of this wacky, wonderful place.

As Tom walked me to my car, I was excited telling him how inspired the show had made me to do that with my blog, to bring this place to life for people who couldn't be here and accurately represent it for the locals. He stopped short and looked at me under the dim streetlight. He wasn't smiling. "Be careful who you share this place with."

I wasn't sure what to say. "Nobody reads it anyway."

"I'm serious. This place is special and it's up to us to keep it that way. Just be careful." He kissed me and held my car door for me. "Get home safely, Slim."

I put the car into first gear and watched him go back into the house in my rearview. Was I an L.A. person in their eyes? In Tom's eyes? Maybe my blogging seemed like putting my diary on the internet to him. Maybe to them I was just another outsider trying desperately to feel local. But as I pulled up to the house my family had built over a century ago, calm washed over me. I was home.

Chapter 8

It was a beautiful day with a balmy breeze carrying the promise of a humid summer. I had all but given up on driving now that the weather was so pleasant. I was walking so often that my body was becoming like a lanky teen's again, despite my new diet of buttery, rich foods.

I was beginning to notice changes in people's homes and gardens. My mom was always saying things like, "The Walters' got a new azalea." I never understood the point. Now, I could see how much those details revealed. You could tell who had children, who'd cut up their manor home and rented it as units like we had, who were avid Saints fans and who loved decorating their house for all occasions. If Mom had been with me, I would have pointed to the house with the giant pink bow on the front door and said, "Looks like it's a girl."

I passed the statue of Margaret, The Bread Woman of New Orleans and marveled at the intricate carving of her crocheted shawl. How in the world did anyone carve all those holes between the weave without breaking the stone? How did they smooth the stone yarn into something gentle and soft? An orphan looked up at her wide, plain face. Margaret had devoted herself to the care of the poor. I liked that her generosity and humility were reason enough to erect a statue. I liked that New Orleans was the kind of city that valued and celebrated kindness. And I loved that it was the first city in America to erect a statue for a woman. There were more too, like Mahalia Jackson's swaying figure singing to the heavens and Saint Joan victoriously hefting her flag on horseback with two cannons leading her way. I kept finding ways this place valued women, ways Los Angeles hadn't. My blood rushed a little with pride or support or something.

I'd been to this building a couple of times for auditions but this was my first time going in for work. That made my blood rush a little too. There was something about diving into the unknown every time a new job started. It didn't matter how many fittings I'd done, how many trailers I'd settled into, how many casts and crews I'd met and how many characters I'd played, there were always far more unknowns than knowns. I had to hand it to the actors who'd created the union rules decades ago that offered some version of a routine. Something as simple as knowing when meal time was gave a sense of structure to our wacky world. Lunch was always six hours after work started, even if that meant we were eating "lunch" at three in the morning.

Printer paper taped to the walls offered arrows to the wardrobe department. No one was sitting at the reception desk, or any of the desks for that matter. "Hello?" I wandered past a rack of tuxedos divided with handmade cardboard markers indicating the film's characters. "Hello?"

"Oh hey! In here."

An arm waved from inside a room. I passed racks

of gowns and sexy athletic wear, shoeboxes piled high and two stacks of fedoras, then pushed the door open. The smiling blonde woman with a salad balanced on her lap didn't get up as I entered. She covered her full mouth and extended her other hand, "Wendy. You're Charlotte?"

"Yes." I put my crocheted backpack down and sat on the chair she indicated with her fork.

"Sorry. The last appointment ran late. Guy had no freaking idea what his sizes were. I don't think he got one measurement right. I'd bought all the wrong stuff and wasted over an hour figuring out I have to go back to the store."

"That's a pain."

"Yeah, looks like I got you right, though. See, a pro knows. You gotta know your sizes."

Now I was beginning to wonder if I'd gotten all my sizes right. "They've changed lately though, right? Vanity sizing. Don't lie to me, you know?"

"He said his shoe was an ten. Then he has these little feet. That's some serious vanity sizing."

"He wanted his feet to look bigger? Maybe his wife buys his clothes."

"Maybe he's an idiot."

We laughed.

"Maybe."

The dresses were beautiful. Regal and feminine. Wendy clearly had a good eye for the festive elegance of a New Orleans cocktail party. I noticed I would put a little more effort into the casual photo poses when I liked a dress more than the others. I had no reason to believe it would help the director choose one of my favorites, but I couldn't see how it would hurt.

The sun was setting as Tom and I walked through the Treme with a group of his friends. We crossed under the whirring overpass to the colorfully painted Ernie K-Doe's Mother-in-Law Lounge. I couldn't get the refrain of the familiar song for which it was named out of my head. We walked through a floral arch, paid our $10 all-you-can-eat cover charge and entered the giant yard out back. A Tiki-hut-like stage sat against the chain link fence at the back property line. Astroturf created a boiling area surrounded by alternating purple and green cast-iron bathtubs planted with flowers and succulents. It was part magical, part garish and all wonderful.

I followed Tom into the sparse lounge. A jukebox played Al Green. Tom greeted the woman behind the bar then led me to a display. A shrine actually. A mannequin of the original owner wearing a stylish pumpkin suit sat in a throne-like chair. "Emperor of the Universe, meet Charlotte. Charlotte, Ernie K-Doe."

"That's crazy. Who made this?"

"His widow, Miss Antoinette."

His wig was perfectly styled framing his face and curling down his shoulders. Someone clearly maintained this character's appearance. The whole thing seemed like an expensive tribute. "What for?"

He laughed. "Oh she kept Mr. Ernie busy. She took him with her everywhere she went, even Commander's Palace for supper."

I looked at some of the memorabilia and photos bedecking the walls and found the dainty, smiling Miss Antoinette with her matching distinctive short-

Farrah-waves-in-front-long-in-back hairdo. It was a strange hairdo for anyone to choose so it seemed to mean something that they could agree on it. They wore matching bedazzled clothing in some of the aged photos. They seemed to agree on what was fun.

I tried to picture Miss Antoinette as an older woman dining with her "husband" at Commander's. Did she talk to him? Did the staff? I was certain they made the couple feel welcome, despite one of them being a doll-person. I was certain the whole city made them feel welcome. I'd seen a movie like that. Ryan Gosling fell in love with a mannequin and his whole town just indulged it. I remember it made me happy-cry thinking of the beauty of that - of this small town tacitly agreeing to let this kind and vulnerable young man live out his delusion of being in a partnership with someone who loved him and needed him.

I pictured Miss Antoinette pushing her "husband" around in a wheelchair, dressing him, combing his hair, watching TV with him. Why not indulge it? Why should she feel the full weight of her loss? Maybe it wasn't even a little crazy. Or maybe it was just my kind of crazy, a crazy I could get behind.

"When Miss Antoinette passed last year, they had a second line, of course, and she had this beautiful funeral carriage with the oval glass sides where you can see the casket inside. And behind that was the family carriage with Mr. Ernie sitting by himself."

"Wait, the mannequin rode alone behind her?"

"Yes and God bless."

I laughed. "That's hilarious. And kinda perfect."

"She'da liked it. It was a big send-off too."

"Well, he was the Emperor of the Universe, so she'd be an Empress, right?"

"Yeah, you right."

I smiled. "I think I love that story. It's kind of ridiculously romantic."

He nodded his head toward the door. "C'mon Slim, let's check out the band." I followed him toward the live music outside, past a giant vat of crawfish boiling and over to a wooden picnic table where our gang gathered. A purple sink, a washing machine and a van emblazoned with, "IT'S FINGER POPPIN' TIME" all sat to the left of the Tiki stage. Breezes carried the spicy steam past our noses and we kept an eye on the meal's progress.

The band finished their set and we all found places around the long tables covered in newspaper. Everyone talked about the crawfish size and the winter weather being so cold. The boiler named Shaggy shook the last of a laundry basket down the middle of the table in front of me. I immediately looked for a corn cob to set aside. It was becoming common for me to eat with strangers here. We'd have to negotiate splitting things like baskets of assorted breads, or in this case – who'd get the corn cobs and potatoes because there wouldn't be enough for everyone. Sometimes it seemed like everything here was designed to create and support community. In L.A., so much of what went on socially happened behind velvet ropes and security men with lists.

After all the crawfish were gone, we had a round of beers back at the picnic table and listened to the band play a few originals. Then Shaggy yelled out "Get 'em while they're hot!" and we all crowded the newspaper-covered tables again for more crawfish. I'd given up on trying to straighten my hair anymore and the breeze kept blowing curls into my mouth. I tried pushing them back with the back of my seasoning-encrusted hand.

Tom motioned to my pile of shells and corn cobs. "You're slowing down."

"It's all the corn. I love the corn."

"Makes my lips burn."

"Yeah, but in a good way." My burning lips smiled. "So, Mom and Julia get here day after tomorrow. I'm not sure what night, but we're planning to go to Commander's for supper. Care to join?"

He pinched another crawfish. "Not exactly a casual setting. Puts kind of a spin on things."

"No, it's not like that. Julia really wants to go now that she's a teenager. She's bringing a dress and kitten heels and she's all excited for our dress-up dinner. It'll be fun."

"Sounds like ladies' night to me."

He did have a point. I ate another crawfish. "Okay, forget that. We're going to get beignets at some point, maybe go to City Park. You're welcome to join for whatever." I sounded like I used to when I was trying to sound like a cool person in L.A., like, "whatever." Crap, I even said "whatever." But, he was right, Commander's was too big for an opener. And it did sound more fun as a girls' night out for three generations.

"Keep me posted. You can text me."

Was he being cagey? Or was I just too used to people paralyzed by fear of commitment? Maybe it was both. I didn't bother asking about the premiere again.

We all headed back to Boudoux's together and Tom walked me to my car. We kissed for a few minutes then he pulled away. "I don't want us to get mugged."

"No, me neither." We weren't joking. I slipped into the front seat. "I'll let you know what we end up doing so you can join us at some point."

"Goodnight Slim. Drive safely." He leaned in and kissed me again then closed the car door. He waved at my rearview and a smile shot across my lips. Then I heard my phone make crickets sounds. At the stop sign, I checked the text. "Night Slim. Sweet dreams." Maybe everything was fine. Maybe I was damaged goods who couldn't trust her instincts anymore. When I first moved, I thought dozens of men were hitting on me, but it turned out they were being polite and friendly. It made me feel like maybe I could be my polite-and-friendly-self without fearing men would think I was hitting on them.

The house seemed darker than usual and I slid my hand down the hallway looking for the switch. The chandelier was lifeless as I kicked my shoes off and donned slippers. I turned on the TV, grabbed my script and a pen and plopped onto the loveseat. I wouldn't be shooting until after Mom's visit, but I knew I wouldn't have the time, privacy or focus to work on the part while they were in town.

I liked that my character was named Cassandra. That was Sassy's real name before Mom's toddler mispronunciations re-dubbed her. I looked up at the photo of Sassy with my cousin's child on her lap and felt warmth. She'd loved and helped raise so many generations of our family.

The name was sometimes a good place to start in building a character. This character was Madame Cassandra, owner of the manor home and hostess of the black-tie party where the movie's stars were planning a heist. They were after a Rodin bronze in my home. Maybe Rodin made a sculpture named Cassandra. I'd look that up too.

Cassandra was a prophetess in Greek mythology. Daughter of Hecuba. Sister of Paris. Wait. Sassy's brother was Paris. Could Mama Heck be short for Hecuba? How odd, though. I wondered aloud, "Why would the daughter of a slave know Greek mythology?" Maybe it was a coincidence. Maybe Mama Heck was short for Hectoria or something. Or maybe it was just the word, like naming your kid Dang.

It had been awhile since I heard that familiar clinking down the hall. The chandelier was at it again. I resisted the urge to check it out and scrolled further. Cassandra was the twin of brother Helenus. Helen was my mother's name but I didn't bother pulling that thought-thread. Cassandra was sent to Elysian Fields by river, like Moses. We paraded Sassy down Elysian Fields during her funeral second line parade, as she requested. It was her most clear demand after the insistence that the chandelier remain in the family and always hang, never sit.

When Cassandra rebuffed the god Apollo's advances, he cursed her with the ability to prophecy but the affliction that no one would believe her. That would suck - always being right and no one believing you. So frustrating. And you'd have to watch them all go through preventable things. Awful.

It took some digging to find her children's names, Teledamus and Pelops. Though they were twins, I didn't feel the need to ask why Sassy didn't use those names for the girls.

Hecuba was the Queen of Troy in Homer's *Iliad*. The stories had variations depending on which site I was reading, but they all agreed she was enslaved by the hero, Odysseus. Some said she escaped by turning herself into a dog. She was the daughter of Eunoe. "Whoa." This was getting freaky. That was Sassy's grandmother's name. Now, I kinda had to know Mama Eunoe's mother's name. The only thing I knew about her was she was a slave but maybe one of the twins would know. I'd call and ask Taffy.

The first thing that came up was a river in Dante's *Divine Comedy*. In Purgatory, the souls reached the Garden of Eden at the top of Mount Purgatory on their journey to God. They washed the memory of their sins in the river Lethe then passed through Eunoe to have the memory of their good deeds strengthened.

I leaned back on the couch and stared up at the ceiling. I saw a mother looking into her baby Eunoe's innocent eyes. She knew what it was like to feel heavy with life's burdens and wanted a name that would wash away the memory of her enslavement and strengthen her good memories. But how would she know these Greek names? What the heck was her name? Was it Greek as well? Odd that they weren't Biblical given they'd come from a southern plantation. If they knew the story, why would Mama Eunoe name her daughter Hecuba knowing her story was about being enslaved by the hero?

The chandelier crystals rattled. Would they do that when Mom and Julia were here? Maybe I wanted a flutter or two. More witnesses to Mama Heck's mischief. I went back to reading. Someone named Matilda would help the souls on their journey. Maybe that was Eunoe's mother's name. But there had to be someone actually named Eunoe in Greek mythology since she was Hecuba's mother. I tried a new search.

Eunoe was a nymph, the daughter of a river god. Some thought her mother might be Persephone. Seemed an unlikely choice for Mama Eunoe's mother's name, but maybe Taffy or Chiffon already knew all of this. I remembered back to Sassy's will reading, her wanting the twins' names to mean something. Why didn't she name them Cassandra and Helen? Maybe she felt weird about naming a child after herself, especially since they weren't originally her children.

I hadn't really found anything useful for the character of Madame Cassandra, but I closed the laptop and turned the TV off. I'd forgotten about the chandelier so I jumped when I turned on the light and found it swinging in a circle like a pendulum. That was new.

Chapter 9

The New Orleans airport was so much more user-friendly than LAX. I spotted Mom and Julia right away. We dropped off their bags and headed straight for the Quarter. Mom and I agreed we should get Julia's curiosity about Bourbon Street out of the way. It was a bright, warm day and the streets weren't cleaned as frequently post-Katrina so the stench of skunked beer and sun-baked vomit wafted up in sporadic breezes. Mom and I exchanged a glance when Julia held her nose. Seemed we were succeeding in dampening young Julia's desire to get old enough to party here.

I stopped in front of Fat Catz and pointed inside. "This is it. This is the place where Taffy and Chiffon's birth mother used to dance."

Julia peeked inside at the cover band playing Earth, Wind & Fire. "Those are Sassy's twins? Taffy and Chiffon?"

Mom swayed to *September*. "Charlotte helped them find their birth mother. She was a dancer here when this was a burlesque house."

Julia turned back to me. "Did they meet?"

"No, I only found her name and a photo. And a little about what she was like, most of which I told the twins. They seemed satisfied with it. I was shocked I found out that much. I've never even played a detective on TV. I was an F.B.I. agent once but that was mostly a lot of chasing and disguises."

Mom laughed. "The *Charlie's Angels* School of Detective Work."

"Pretty much."

Without speaking, we all dropped into angel-with-gun poses then laughed too loud. A tall, sturdy man with a bushy mustache walked past wearing dark sunglasses and a cowboy hat pulled over a yellow curly wig, a black bikini top with gold sequin trim, a black and gold tutu and cowboy boots. We watched him pass then looked back to each other and laughed all over again.

Mom explained the history of things to Julia as we headed to the art galleries and chandelier shops of Royal Street. I led them to the windows of M.S. Rau, an antique store I'd passed many times and never entered. "This place always has the craziest things in the windows. Look." I led them to a window displaying a crystal throne with purple velvet cushioning. "Right?"

Julia stepped to the pane of glass and made a visor of her hands. "Are you kidding me? Whose house does this make sense in? And you just buy the one? So like, everyone else is sitting in chairs and you're sitting in this?"

Mom mocked sitting in the chair and waving her arm past us majestically. "Make yourself at home."

"We have to go in." Julia led us back to the front door.

I didn't hurry. "You may need an appointment. Did you notice a sign on the door?"

But she and Mom were already inside. To the left

was a super-long room with elaborate chandeliers cluttering the ceiling. Below them were long tables exhibiting cut-crystal bowls, vases and decanters. In front of us was an even longer room with jewelry cases lining the right wall. Each beautifully lit piece looked unique, regal and beyond expensive. They looked to be museum-quality pieces.

A tall brunette with a wide smile stepped behind the counter to serve us. "It's David Morris. The necklace." We all took interest in his accent as he pointed at a dazzling three-strand diamond necklace. Russian? French? What was that accent?

Mom leaned in. "My word, that's too much."

"It's 72.58 Carats."

I smiled at the man with the confusing accent. "It's stunning. Mom just doesn't like fancy things."

The man smiled at Julia. "How about you? Do you like fancy things?" She nodded. "Follow me." He smiled at her. "I'm Ludovic."

"I'm Julia. How much did that necklace cost, Ludovic?"

Mom tugged her sleeve. "Julia."

"It's okay. Everything has a price here. That necklace is $885,000, Julia." We followed him past smaller rooms filled with fancy collectibles, through a darkened hallway lined with statues and through to much larger rooms filled with antique furniture, clocks and musical instruments. We followed him to a towering golden clock inlaid with colorful and exotic flowers and maybe an archer on a horse?

"This is a clock made in 1745 by Jean-Pierre Latz for Augustus III, King of Saxony and Poland. And before you ask, it's priced at $1,250,000."

We lingered to take it all in as he moved across the room. "This way. This is a fun one." We hurried to join him, passing dozens of extraordinary items. "An Ice Age cave bear skeleton."

The skeleton with its long spine and short legs stood over eight feet tall. I tried to picture owning this piece of history. Where did someone display an Ice Age cave bear skeleton? The living room? It seemed more of a den thing. By a fireplace maybe.

Ludovic left us to wander through all the pricey pieces. There were paintings by Chagall, Cassatt and Toulouse-Lautrec. A collection of antique walking canes were topped with sculpted and jeweled handles. There were magical carousel horses, carved white jade vases and royalty-worthy jewels from Cartier, Tiffany and Van Cleef & Arpels.

We waved to Ludovic and thanked him as we exited. Julia took a last glance at the windows as we walked Royal. "Who buys stuff there?"

Mom laughed. "Rich people."

I smiled. "Collectors. People with refined taste. And people who want to show off. But I would imagine they do business globally. They have to have a website or auctions or something because those pieces were crazy. For that not to be a museum? That was amazing. And that guy didn't seem to mind we had no kinda money for him."

Mom grabbed my waist. "Maybe he could tell you have a lot of rich friends."

"I prefer fancy."

Julia slowed to watch a man standing on a ladder that seemed suspended against an invisible wall. A piece of lumber balanced on his shoulder. "I want fancy friends when I get older. Then you get to see all those collectibles no one else gets to see."

"That's actually true. I thought you were going to say something... not as observant. I once watched a movie in a guy's house who had the largest private art collection in the world. He had a Monet *Waterlilies*, a Picasso, a Lichtenstein and bronzes by Botero and my favorite, Rodin. And the whole time I was there, I kept thinking I was one of a handful of people that got to see these museum pieces. I felt very privileged, but I also felt like it was somehow exclusive. Like it excluded other art lovers, students and people who hadn't yet fallen in love with art. But if you're gonna spend giant chunks of money on something, I totally get wanting to have a Rodin I can see everyday. That makes sense to me."

Mom gave Julia a dollar to give the man on the ladder after she'd taken a picture of him. "I wouldn't even know how to spend money like that. If I ever won the lottery, I'd give you the money and let you spend it, Charlotte."

Julia dropped the dollar in his can and caught up to us. "I'm hungry."

Excited, Mom clapped her hands together. "Aren't we near that place with the balcony?"

"Ain't der no mo'. It never made it back after The Storm. There's a shop there now, Forever New Orleans. Sells nice NOLA-centric stuff. Stuff even locals would buy."

Mom dropped her hands. "No more one-man-band playing below the balcony?"

"I haven't seen him. Maybe he moved. Or passed. He was pretty old even back then. But I know a place with a wonderful grilled shrimp and asparagus salad topped with crab meat."

Julia yelled, "Sold!"

We had missed the lunch crowd at Muriel's so most of the rustic dining room was nearly empty. The majority of faces peered from old-world portraits on the wall. As always, the service was friendly and knowledgeable, and the salads were as tasty as I'd bragged they'd be. Outside the window, dozens of kids in yellow t-shirts filed out of buses and into Jackson Square. "Wait! I think I know who this is. I think those are those kids I told you about who I saw playing with an adult band at one of the free Wednesday concerts. Roots something."

"Oh yes." Mom's hands were clapped together again.

"It's a kids band?" Julia was staring at the steady stream of kids walking past the window. "How old are they? They look so young."

I jumped up from my chair. "Maybe they're gathering in the Square to play! Let's go. Maybe y'all can see them. I would love that." Now I was the one clapping.

But the kids weren't assembling. They were disappearing into the Cabildo, one of the museums on the Square. A super-tall man in a blue t-shirt imprinted with the "The Roots of Music" logo seemed to be in charge.

"Hey, do you know if the kids are going to play somewhere today? My mother and niece just got here today and I'd love for them to see them perform. I told them how amazing the band is."

His voice was low and slow like a sexy lulluby.

"They play here everyday. This is where they practice."

"Seriously? Cool place to practice."

"You wanna see it? The kids should be getting started."

Julia smiled wide. "Can we? That would be cool."

He extended his large hand. "I'm Derrick. I came up with this after The Storm when I saw how little there was for kids who stayed."

I interrupted. "Wait, this is your band?"

"I remembered how much my band leader influenced me when I was comin' up and thought - that's somethin' I can do. So I got this great partner and we started Roots of Music together. Now we have over a hundred kids in the program, eight to thirteen. And five hundred more kids on the wait list." He nodded to the woman at the admissions desk. "They're with me." She smiled, nodded and went back to her papers.

We followed Derrick through a courtyard and into a back room where beginners were learning horns. Something about "no excuses" was written on the chalkboard. He spoke softly. "We provide the instruments, teach 'em to read music. They learn about rests and quarter notes, stuff. Y'all play anything?"

Julia was excited to tell Derrick she'd begun playing drums with her school band about a year ago. I'd always pitied the parents of drummers. The teacher was helping the kids with posture, breathing and proper arm placement.

Derrick tapped my arm and we followed him up a elegantly winding staircase to the intermediate horn players. We stayed and listened awhile then circled another flight to the tuba players. Those always impressed me the most in parades - sousaphonists and big bass drummers. The parades were miles long and often in inclement weather. I couldn't imagine being able to carry such a huge instrument that many miles at that young an age. Heck, I couldn't imagine even picking a tuba up and lifting it over my head and onto my shoulder.

Derrick led us back down the stairs and into a room packed with kids sitting on the floor with drum pads. The teacher was as strict and focused as the other instructors but harder to please as he drilled the students and prepped them to play.

Julia leaned to my ear and whispered, "If he was my teacher, I wouldn't like him."

"Just wait."

"It's discouraging, don't you think? What's the point of being so strict? It can be more fun."

I got on my tiptoes and whispered to Derrick, "Are they just going to do exercises or will we hear them play?"

"They'll play."

"Oh yay!" I stifled a clap.

Half a dozen boys stood with drums hanging at their waists. The teacher said technical things the kids seemed to understand and, on command, they sharply lifted their sticks across their chests like military men displaying weapons. Derrick pointed to the three year old at the end of the line-up. "He's mine."

Mom looked like she was watching fireworks made of rainbows. Julia was frozen with her mouth slightly open. The boys played like soulful machines ratatat-tatting rapid-fire on their own drums then crossing sticks as they playing the drum beside them. The discipline involved in their showmanship and the attention to detail required made for a stunning sight. Mom swung her arms like she was marching along with them in a Mardi Gras parade.

The three year old performed a solo and Julia leaned over to whisper again. She pointed her nose toward him and nodded. "He's better than everyone in my band, including me."

"Yeah but this is a town where Trombone Shorty and Harry Connick Jr. played at that age. You don't get points for being a baby here – if you can play, you can play. Period."

Julia never took her eyes off the drummers as more and more joined in, emphasizing the precision and discipline it took to execute this rehearsal. "I could be so good if he was my teacher."

"Yeah, wouldn't that be fun?"

She smiled slightly, still intent on their fancy drumstick tricks and insane playing. "Yeah."

Derrick led us out and back into Jackson Square where a brass band played for tips. "In this city, you know how to play, you can make a livin'. I started right there where they playin'." He looked toward the brass band spread around the metal benches with a semi-circle of tourists around them. "Lots of us did."

Mom jumped in. "Charlotte has a blog. Maybe she'll mention your kids." I hated when Mom spoke for me but she was right to bring it up. I clearly hadn't.

He handed me a card. "You're a writer?"

Mom jumped in again. "She's a famous actor."

"Mom!" I hated when I went full-teen in reaction to her.

Derrick smiled. "You do plays?" There it was again. At least he didn't go with, "Which restaurant?" Here, actor seemed to equal artist. Though it often left me feeling like I had to explain myself, I kinda liked people assuming I was serious about my craft. It mattered even more coming from someone who clearly understood how much hard work and discipline it took to appear effortlessly talented.

"Mostly TV and film. Gotta pay the bills."

"I hear ya."

"But Mom's exaggerating. If someone's actually famous, you don't really need to ask who they are, right? I just work a lot."

That seemed to be enough for him so we said our goodbyes and headed toward Café du Monde for beignets. The setting sun brought a new group of vendors to the Square. Fortune tellers abounded. Julia squealed. "Can we get a reading?"

I wasn't a big fan but if she thought it'd be fun, I couldn't see the harm. "Which one do you want?"

She surveyed the soothsayers. Most sat behind card tables covered in scarves and topped with a lit candle. The one that had been there all day was closing a beach umbrella they'd been using for shade. Julia wandered toward a rounded woman with short blonde curls and a slightly mischievous smile. "Stella" was painted on a chalkboard and surrounded by painted stars. Stella's dress looked like it was made of scarves, shiny things and mermaid dreams. "Five dollars for a reading. Tarot or palm. I've got runes too if you're partial to that sort of thing. I'll do all three of you for fifteen and consider myself tipped."

It was too good a deal for them to pass up so I went along. We took turns sitting on the foldout chair. It seemed most of Mom's trials were behind her. I wanted to believe that so badly. And Julia had a bright future owing to her cornucopia of talents and interests. Her greatest task was to find her path, as there seemed little doubt she would achieve any goals she set for herself. As a biased aunt, I was glad Julia was hearing all of this from a stranger - someone she might actually listen to without fear of familial coddling or flattery.

The chair was still warm when I took my turn. I closed my eyes and prayed silently. "God, if there's something you want me to know, I'm paying attention right now. Use this woman for my best good."

Stella shuffled the tarot cards and placed them in front of me to cut several times. Then she laid out a grid three-by-three. "You've returned to your soulmate."

Mom let out a little "woooo."

I couldn't help wondering if she was talking about Tom.

"He's older maybe. He's a great communicator so I think he's older. You really need that. You like talking things out, figuring things out. You need a great communicator."

I wouldn't have called Tom a "great communicator" and he was actually younger than I was, something we discovered a bit late in the game. "You're an all-in kinda girl. You want to meet your match and be in it with him. He's a workaholic, but you don't mind because it's for a cause you believe in." I did care about the environment but I wouldn't have called Tom a workaholic.

Stella turned over another card and placed it across one of the cards. "Your career just goes zoom in a couple years. 2012? Everything you've been working toward comes together then." She flipped another card. "And you marry after that. It's a good marriage. Not like the one in your youth."

Lucky guess.

She looked up at me. "You've returned. And this is good. But, you're scratching at scabs." She took my hand and held it between hers. "Be careful what you wish for - don't ask questions you don't want the answers to."

I felt a small shiver.

"It says you are The Protector."

Julia looked at the cards. "Of what?"

Stella looked straight into me. "She knows." Then she let my hand go. Mom gave Stella a twenty and thanked her.

Mom and Julia talked about their futures as we grabbed a table at Café du Monde for beignets and hot chocolate.

Mom and I pulled several inadequately-sized napkins from the dispenser on the table and spread them to cover our clothes. Julia giggled. "Planning to spill something?"

Mom laughed and handed her some napkins. "It's for the sugar, sugah." The waitress in the paper hat placed the thick white-enameled cups and saucers in front of us, then sat the plates of beignets between us. Mom was first to take one and gave herself a powdered sugar mustache biting into the pillow of fried dough. "It doesn't matter how many times I eat these, each time I think it can't possibly be as good as I remember. Then, each time it's even better. How can that be?"

Julia looked skeptical. "It's fried dough, right? Like a churro or a funnel cake?"

Mom finished chewing. "It's a French donut, darlin'."

Julia took a bite and her face lit up. "Oh my God. This is so good. I thought you guys were being nostalgic or something. Oh my God. This is so good."

Mom smiled, chewing.

"Aunt Charlotte, what do you think that lady meant by, 'You are the protector?'"

I felt suddenly goofy. I didn't even have to rehearse it in my head, I knew how crazy it would all sound. "I don't know. She's a street performer."

Mom dabbed her lips with a paper napkin. "Oh honey. She said you knew. What are you protecting?"

I tapped sugar off my beignet and took a bite, chewing it slowly. "Okay, but you have to promise you'll still sleep in the house even if it's a spooky story."

Mom waved her napkin. "Oh no. I don't think I can promise that. Did someone die there?"

"Mother, it's New Orleans. Someone died right here. Seriously. One of the producers of that new TV show *Treme* died right here just a while ago."

"Lordy."

Julia put her cup down. "Seriously?"

"That would be a pretty weird thing to make up. So, can we just leave it alone now?"

Julia shook her head. "I still wanna hear."

"Oh, lordy."

I spooned an ice cube out of my water glass and rubbed it between my hands then wiped them with small, tissuey napkins. "It's the chandelier, but I'm not the protector, Mama Heck is."

Mom laughed and powdered sugar puffed from her mouth. "Darlin', Mama Heck's been gone a long time. That was Sassy's mother, Julia. She raised my mother."

"I know Mom." There went that teen-agitation voice again. I took a breath. "The chandelier does weird things. I debated on telling you but it hangs over the bed y'all'll be sleepin' in so you may as well know."

They both said "What kind of weird things?" at the same time, but Julia's voice sounded excited and Mom's sounded cautious.

"Nothing bad. It just moves. On it's own."

Mom looked genuinely concerned. "Moves how?"

"I don't know. Like, sometimes it swings."

Mom smiled. "Sweetie, this ground is like gelatin. It's probably just a truck passing."

"Sometimes just one crystal will stick out. Suddenly. Like in front of you."

Julia was into it. "That's weird. But why do you have to protect it? Or Mama Heck or whatever."

"I have no idea. I just know the rules. It has to stay in the family and it always has to hang."

Mom looked confused. "Our family or Sassy's family? Doesn't it belong to the twins now?"

"They didn't have anywhere to hang it, so they

were hoping hanging it in what was once their family home would be close enough. Wasn't Mama Heck born there or raised there or whatever?"

"Yes. Until she got the Treme house."

Julia waved her hand once. "Wait, why does it have to hang?"

"Beats me."

Mom seemed surprised. "You have no idea? Not even a guess?"

"Yeah, you always have some theory or opinion. Guess something."

They were both looking at me with faces that said, We know you.

"There was one thing."

Mom and Julia high-fived powdery fingers.

"Okay, fine. When Taffy and UncaParis brought it to the house, it was on the ground for a minute while he got the wires ready and there was some crunchy, old masking tape on the top part, the fixture part that goes to the ceiling. I kinda pulled it off and there were some initials carved there and a symbol." I had their undivided attention even as birds were gathering around our feet to peck at crumbs. "It was scratched and written in kinda fancy script so I'm just guessing, but I'm thinking the initials were LW DW. Or SW OW."

"And what was the symbol of?" Julia copied my ice cube trick.

"I honestly have no idea. But Mom, do you remember that pipe Dad had? It was the same symbol carved into his pipe."

"His pipe? What are you saying?"

"I have no idea. It could just be a brand."

She looked doubtful. "A pipe and chandelier brand?"

"And flasks. I found it on a flask too, at what used to be a brothel."

Mom placed her napkins on the table and slapped at her pants as she stood. "Sounds like it's fairly common for the era."

"Maybe so."

Julia pushed her chair in. "Really? Not even Walmart has flasks, pipes and chandeliers."

I laughed. "You sure about that?"

We walked up the ramp and crossed the tracks to the river. Julia started down the steps ahead of us. "Careful!"

Julia yelled over her shoulder. "Yeah, I know - someone died here too, right?"

"A kid fell in and probably drowned a week or so ago." I looked at Mom. "Well, he did. They haven't found him yet, but it looks like he just fell in and died."

"That's horrible." She looked out at the dark river glistening with reflected city lights. "I don't want you scaring Julia with ghost stories. It can be hard to sleep in an unfamiliar environment."

"I don't know what to say, Mom. Either it'll happen while y'all are here or it won't. Either way, I'm stickin' to my story."

"Well sugah, you and I've seen stranger. Guess we'll wait and see."

Before heading home, we walked to Frenchmen Street so they could hear some local music. I loved watching Mom dance in the streets with abandon. Julia seemed self-conscious so we grabbed her hands and helped her give in. This was among my mother's greatest gifts to me, her willingness to experience joy publicly. I hated it as a teen, thought it was embarrassing. And I secretly envied it, which made me even more stiff and frustrated. By the time I was eighteen, I let my hips sway and my hair fly and I never looked back.

When we got back to the house, there was teasing about the chandelier but they got settled into bed and I headed to the living room's pull-out couch. I found Derrick's card and looked him up online. Many of the links were for sites and articles about Rebirth Brass Band. I clicked one and found a photo of the band, but it was too small. I went to my blog, searched "Rebirth" and clicked on a post with plenty of photos. There he was, Derrick Tabb on snare drum.

I started rewinding my conversations with him. Did I say anything ridiculous when we talked about my favorite bands? Did he think I knew who he was? Did he assume I didn't because I said something dorky?

In any case, he was a prince among men. He took us through the Cabildo like it was the chambers of his heart, showing us what mattered most to him – music, community and family. And he was in my favorite brass band. I loved this city.

I checked my email and bolted upright when I saw the one saying my shoot date had been moved up to tomorrow afternoon. I had a whole day planned with Mom and Julia. Now, I had a call time at four. At least we'd get the morning together.

Chapter 10

After brunch, we walked around the Garden District and Mom told Julia stories about growing up there, about living so close to the parade route and about who lived in which house when she was a kid. She named many of the trees and flowers and remembered when some of them had been planted. I saw trucks lining one of the streets. "Hey, I think that's where I'm shooting later. Wanna walk by and see what they're setting up?"

"Cool!" That put a skip in Julia's step.

Someone was unloading director's chairs from the back of a nearly empty truck. A young woman in overalls and a tank top pressed white tape onto the door of a trailer and inscribed it with "Charlie" in black Sharpie. There was a Charlie in my script. "I think this is it." I scanned the lawn and spotted Ethan and Todd. Ethan waved. "It's my happy-ending girl!"

Ugh. "Ethan, this is my mother and my niece. Let's keep it family. Hey Todd. We were just walking by. Hope you don't mind the drop-in."

Ethan became suddenly charming. "Right. Your visit. Sorry we're blowing it for you. We had a scheduling issue with one of our names and had to flip some things." He slapped Todd's arm then pointed back and forth between Mom and Julia. "Hey, party scene, right?"

Todd nodded. "Yeah, sure. We could use the demographics."

"Do you ladies have party dresses? What are you doing today? Do you want to be in a movie?"

Julia looked up at us like a puppy hoping for a walk. "Can we?"

"I would love that. I never even bothered to dream I could work with my family since I'm the only one in the industry."

Mom clapped. "Oh yay! When do we report to work, boss?"

Ethan laughed. "Go get your party dresses and be back for four, camera ready but not in wardrobe. Bring choices if you have them. You'll help them, right Charlotte?"

"On it."

Julia had a million questions on the walk home. It did occur to me that they never asked if Julia was a minor. Fingers crossed that it wouldn't matter.

We bagged their dresses and shoes, helped Julia with her age-appropriate makeup and headed back to the bustling set.

Mom and Julia were escorted to a wardrobe person who would check out their clothes and I followed a P.A. to hair and makeup. "We don't have a trailer for you so when you're done, just head into the house. There's a green room for some of you there." Her walkie squawked. She pushed the button. "Switching to channel three. Hey, yeah, they should already have that by now. I'll be right there." She smiled at me. "You good?" I nodded and she was gone.

The door opened again and a familiar voice said,

"Stepping up. Hey, how's everyone today? Who went out last night since we had a late call today?" I looked in the mirror and saw Bryan Batt over my shoulder just as he took me in. "It's my streetcar buddy." I twisted around and we managed a hug. "Oh, I'm terrible. Remind me your name."

"Charlotte. Oh yay! I'm so glad we get to work together. My mom and niece are doing background too. Best cast ever, so far."

"Your playing the lady of the manor? I'm the scoundrel."

"Of course you are."

The makeup artist looked at Bryan in the mirror. Her voice was much higher than I thought it would be, almost cartoonish. "Did they ever have a memorial for that kid that drowned? Keith? Didn't you work with him once?"

"I can't imagine the family having a memorial without a body. Wouldn't optimism win out?"

She tapped powder from a big, bushy brush. "So, was there a second line?"

"He wasn't a musician. And I didn't get the sense he was wildly popular as a local so I'm guessing no."

The hairdresser working on me piped up. "You gotta play or pay. But that kid was an odd bird. Dudn't anybody miss him much. Everybody's just curious."

I could see that.

The "green room" was actually the home's beautifully appointed sitting room. Several actors with semi-familiar faces lounged on comfy oversized sofas. An original Blue Dog hung on the wall. Everyone was talking about the catering and when "lunch" would be. As much as I felt like a fish out of water in L.A., I always felt right at home on a set. Ethan led fully-dressed Mom and Julia in. "You guys can wait here for - Charlotte! Don't they look beautiful?"

They did. It was fun sharing the magic and tedium with Mom and Julia. Bryan made them feel like belles of the ball as we all waited for the sun to finally set over the live oaks so we could begin shooting.

During blocking, they put Mom and Julia in a grouping with me near the pool. Though neither of them would be able to speak, Todd gave Julia an entrance and some business. We shot the scene a few times before someone yelled, "Moving on. Turning around."

Mom looked at me. "What does that mean?"

Bryan answered as he passed. "It means we have a break."

I smiled at Julia. "It means they're setting up to do the same scene from a different angle."

Bryan paused as Julia seemed to be calculating. "So you guys have to do everything you just did again with the same emotions and everything but after you take a break? Is that hard?"

Bryan laughed. "That's the job. Hard but wonderful." A good-looking guy wearing Bryan's exact same outfit walked up. "My better half! This is my stuntman, Trevor."

Trevor was clearly younger but they were a great match.

I extended my hand. "Charlotte. I love stunts."

Julia seemed to think he was cute.

We chatted and waited inside until they came for us again. Everyone resumed their first positions and ran the scene again as they shot us from another angle. Between takes, I thought I saw someone beyond the bushes peering in. Probably a nosy neighbor. A few takes later, I noticed him again. "Mom, do you see that? Do you see someone out there? I feel like there's someone lurking. Is he part of the scene?"

Bryan leaned from his grouping to ours. "Someone's lurking?"

"There, past the bushes. Do you see him?"

Bryan struggled to see past the foliage. "Trevor" Trevor snapped to attention then joined us. "Can you go look through those bushes and see if there's someone lurking out there?"

"Like a stalker?"

I interjected. "It's probably just a passer-by but it's not a bad idea to check."

Trevor walked toward the bushes and we could hear someone running away. Trevor grabbed a low branch and pulled himself up to see over the bushes. Bryan looked around to see who was watching. "Trevor, your wardrobe."

He jumped down. "Sorry. He's gone now, whoever it was. I wouldn't worry about it."

Everyone snapped back into motion. Mom and Julia were excited to see Trevor's stunt. We watched as the director went through the shot and Trevor nodded a lot. Trevor played it out a few times step-by-step and they seemed to agree on some things.

The First A.D. yelled out to all of us. "We're going to try to get this in one, folks. Once he's wet, there's about a half hour reset we're trying to avoid so everybody be paying attention." He raised his voice. "Background, do not look into the camera and do not anticipate the stunt. Okay, folks, going in two."

Mom looked nervous. "Now I'm afraid I'm going to look into the camera."

"I don't think we're in the shot. I think we get to watch." I pointed. "The camera's over there so if we're in the shot at all, I think your back is to the camera anyway."

The First A.D. yelled again. "Okay people, pay attention. Let's get this in one. And... action!"

I still wasn't sure we were in the shot but chances were good since no one had asked us to move. I pretended to talk and Mom and Julia followed suit. I always silently told a real story rather than just moving my mouth. I couldn't tell which they were doing. Julia mostly smiled.

Then we heard, "Action Trevor!"

Trevor got pushed into the shot, keeping his face slightly away from the camera. I wished I could tell Mom and Julia we called that "cheating." Sometimes we cheated toward the camera. We cheated our eyes, cheated our shoulders, we cheated all sorts of things - but I'd never noticed it in a finished film or TV show. Even after peeking behind the curtain.

Trevor pushed the actor back and we all reacted, stopping our actions to notice the fight. Shouldn't I have been rushing closer at this point, saying something? It was my home, my party. Why hadn't anyone given me an action? I was too afraid to improvise anything knowing we only had one take.

The actor pushed Trevor again and he flew

backward and into the water, covering his face with his arm as he spun away from camera. We all reacted. I was going to have to run toward them, right? It wouldn't make sense for me not to. I cheated my eyes toward the crew standing off to the side hoping to catch a signal from Todd. A few of them were covering their mouths to stifle screams or laughs.

Todd clapped his hands together victoriously. "Cut!" They huddled around a monitor to watch playback.

I was glad we could finally speak softly. "Where they huddle like that around a monitor, we call that 'video village.' I used to think they were all watching the same clip but now I know each department head is only really watching what they're in charge of. Wardrobe only really focuses on the clothing, lighting only really sees the lighting, the script supervisor's watching 'continuity' and on and on. It's fascinatingly myopic."

"What's continuity?" Julia was always the curious type. I loved that.

"If we have lines, she looks to see if we say them all and writes how we actually ended up saying them. If you lift your right arm in one shot and your left arm in another, she'll tell you, tell the director and make a note of it for the editor. She watches whatever you're wearing and notes if you buttoned something differently or whatever. It's an unsung-hero job, and people only notice it when they mess up. A glass is three-quarters full in one shot and full in the next and audiences can end up obsessing over stupid stuff and feeling like they 'caught' us somehow. So, her job is to miss nothing and note everything so when they get in the edit bay, they know what they have in their footage."

The video village gang all shouted versions of "Whoa!" then Todd smiled. "Check the gate." Then he shouted, "Moving on!"

"My five favorite words."

Mom watched everyone jump back into action. "They got it?"

"Yeah, so the rest of the night will probably be less tense now that we got the hard, potentially-expensive part out of the way."

The sound guy was reviewing the clip as we walked past. "Do you mind if they see? It's my mom and niece and it's their first time on a set."

He handed a set of headphones to Mom. "Sure." He gave his own to Julia. "I can start it again but you haven't missed anything yet. Wait, here he comes."

Trevor stumbled into the shot. The pushing looked very convincing. Then Trevor flew back, crossed his arm over his face, and spun away from camera. And though everyone in front of the camera reacted, the camera remained motionless, like a calm voyeur - like the video of the kid drowning. It seemed suddenly unreasonable that anyone could have been behind that camera and not reacted. I wanted to run into the shot when I saw somebody just playacting falling into the water. Wouldn't anyone behind the camera drop it or run into the shot?

So if it was just a camera by itself, was it set up by the missing guy? How did the police find it? No one stole an unattended phone in the grass by the river? Where homeless people slept sometimes? Someone had to know how the cops got that phone.

And why did the kid leave it on the ground facing the exact place he fell in? Was he trying to make a video of himself doing something important or maybe something silly? He must have intended to record himself doing something, right? But at night? Who records themselves doing something memorable in the dark? For what purpose? It bothered me.

"Cool!" Julia smiled and handed her headphones back to the sound man. "Thank you. That was cool."

He smiled. "And it's the only shot we know for sure will be the one they use in the movie. They'll do coverage to get Bryan's face in close-ups and medium shots but that's definitely the footage they'll use of the moment he goes in the water."

Work went long, and because she was a minor, they had to wrap Julia after eight hours. She ended up napping on the couch in our holding room while Mom and I finished out the night. I was glad Julia got to do my scenes with me and actually silent-act a little.

Mom was exhausted when we got home. She wasn't used to being up until three in the morning. I was a little wired so I wrote a little blog about working with Mom and Julia. I was careful not to mention any names or specifics about the film, just that we'd worked together and how it felt to finally share that part of my life with my family.

I posted the blog on my Facebook public page and checked to see how many hits my blog about The Roots of Music had gotten. Sixty-eight. Pretty good. I went back to Facebook and already had a "like." It was the flexed-muscle guy who'd sent me a friend request I'd ignored. I clicked over to his page.

Still no personal information and only a few dozen "friends." It was hard for me to imagine being so isolated. I scrolled through the friends and found Trevor. Small world. Maybe they went to the same gym. Wait, Keith Dalton? D-Man, the flexed-arm guy was friends with the missing guy? Even smaller world.

I scrolled D-Man's timeline. Fitness videos. Muscly memes. A reposting of an article about the drowned kid being presumed dead. Maybe they were actual friends.

I closed the computer and pulled the couch out to finally rest.

Chapter 11

Being an actor opened many doors I'd never imagined from world travel to dating movie stars, but it closed doors too. Scheduling was the biggest and most consistent loss. Had I planned to travel to spend Julia's birthday with her, I would've had to cancel last minute for the movie. Instead, we ended up working on it together. I'd missed many weddings, christenings, graduations and funerals over the years. Having her here meant that not only would I not have to make that dreaded cancellation phone call, we could actually spend the day celebrating Julia's birthday with New Orleans flair.

I rummaged for a safety pin in a crafting drawer then grabbed a five dollar bill from my coin purse and flattened it on the edge of my desk. "Julia!"

She and Mom were donning light sweaters when I entered the bedroom. I held the fiver up. "You're doing this." She stood with her chin turned away as I pinned the money to her chest. "Now everyone will know it's your birthday."

She looked down at the bill. "What do you mean?"

"It's a tradition. You pin money on your chest and throughout the day, people will wish you a happy birthday. Some might even add money to your chest."

Mom smiled. "People still do that?"

"Really? Total strangers?" Julia looked baffled.

I smiled. "You'll see."

I don't think Julia believed me until the first time a passing car slowed so the driver could yell birthday wishes to her. When the valet at Commander's Palace added a dollar, she started to see the advantages but remained confused. "Why do they do it?"

"Pin the money? It's like buying you a drink. To celebrate."

"But they don't even know me."

Mom laughed as we passed under the wrought iron arch of Lafayette Cemetery #1. "Just enjoy it."

I motioned toward the stone mausoleums. "Okay, we can take a tour if you want or just wander. Birthday Girl's choice."

Mom and I were glad she chose wandering. We showed her the many dates that indicated the mass deaths during the Yellow Fever outbreak. Julia was devastated to find entire families dying within days of each other. I was glad the tomb to the orphaned boys hadn't been cleared off for awhile so she could see all the toys and baubles left for them. Mom explained that many people could fit into one of the above-ground tombs, their bodies rotting down to bones making room for more.

"That's so much better for the environment."

I was glad Julia saw it that way and not as some sort of sacrilege.

"Are all these people rich? These tombs are beautiful."

Mom laughed again. "Darlin', we're below sea level. You can't put them in the ground and think they'll stay there."

"Ew, really? They'd pop out of the ground?"

It was my turn to laugh. "Like the pool scene in *Poltergeist*."

"What's Poltergeist?"

Now it was my turn to feel old. "It's a movie."

Mom added, "A scary one. Ghosts haunting a family. And those chairs! Your father and Charlotte stacked our kitchen chairs while I was out seeing the movie. They thought it was hilarious when I nearly choked screaming."

"Come on Mom, they were the same exact chairs. We couldn't resist."

Julia leaned in to read a rain-faded inscription about an immigrant from Germany who'd died in 1879. "Do you really think you have a ghost in your house? We haven't seen anything weird."

"I don't know what to tell you, Julia. Sometimes the chandelier does things I can't explain."

"What do you think it wants?"

I hadn't really asked myself that. "Attention? I don't know." Did it want something from me? "Your mother had a dream about a bookstore where she thought I might meet someone special. Wanna see?"

We headed out of the cemetery and I led them toward the Garden District Book Shop in The Rink shopping center. The nice guy with the gentle face who'd helped me on my last visit greeted us as we wandered in three directions. "Happy birthday!"

I shot Julia a smile.

A woman with red curls came out from behind the counter and Julia allowed her to add a dollar to her collection. "I love this tradition."

"What's not to love? Are you looking for anything

in particular? A present maybe?"

Mom snapped to attention. "Yes! Julia, pick something out. On me."

We ignored the bestsellers and searched the rows of local-centric books. The gentle-faced man helped Julia narrow her search and she settled on a collection of stories about the contributions of women in New Orleans. Though I wanted her to believe me about the chandelier doing things, I was glad she'd picked it over the many books about our best known ghost stories.

We treated ourselves to shrimp and grits for lunch then window-shopped Magazine Street on our way back to the house. Albert was sitting in front of Design Within Reach sipping a paper cup of coffee someone had spotted him. He pushed his long salt-and-pepper dreads back from his face and I hoped his milky eye wouldn't scare Julia.

"Albert! I'm so glad we're crossing paths. This is my mom and my niece. They're visiting."

"Well, look at that. Three generations. Happy birthday. Blessings on your day."

Julia smiled. "Thanks. You too."

He beamed at Mom. "Y'all showing her a good time?"

I jumped in. "We're taking her to the movies. They're showing *The Big Lebowski* tonight at The Prytania."

"The big who?"

Mom laughed. "That's what I said. But Charlotte seems to think she'll love it."

"You already seen it and you gonna see it again? Must be good."

"It's from the late nineties. The Coen brothers. It's kind of a classic."

"I don't go to movies much. Don't know them brothers. Did meet someone from the TV though. Few days ago. Said they liked my look. I told 'em, 'Me too.'"

I loved Albert. "Me too." I hugged him and we all waved our goodbyes and Julia and Mom followed me down the sidewalk. "That's Albert. He was the first friend I made here."

Julia seemed concerned. "He's homeless?"

"I don't think so 'cause he always smells bathed but I've never asked. To be fair, he never asked me where I live either."

Julia looked back at him as he settled back into the chair in front of the shop. "I like him. He's got good energy."

"Goodness yes," Mom agreed.

The chandelier made no moves as we hustled to get ready for the movie. Mom was still dubious about the film choice but she was excited for Julia to see the movie house she'd gone to so frequently as a kid.

It was theme night, but I was the only one of our bunch who donned a bathrobe and sunglasses. I wondered if I'd feel goofy but as we pulled up to the single-screen theatre, the sidewalk was lined with bathrobe-wearing patrons. They were just letting the line in as we got our tickets.

Mom was in a nostalgic haze. "Your father courted me here. When your uncle and I were kids, we'd come to get out of the heat. A nickel a show. We loved the musicals the best. But we'd watch anything to escape the summers."

The guys sitting next to us pulled rum and milk from a cooler on the dingy floor. "White Russian?"

We declined and I explained to Mom and Julia that it was part of the movie. Mom bragged loud enough for the guys to hear. "Charlotte knows the man this movie's based on."

One of the guys nearly dropped his plastic go-cup. "Wait, there's a real Dude? He slapped his friend's arm nearly spilling his drink.

"Careful man, there's a beverage here!"

Mom and Julia didn't get the joke.

"It's a line in the movie." I found myself speaking in Mom's loud-and-proud volume. "Yeah, Jeff Dowd. He lives in L.A. We met at a premiere when he let me sit with him and his date."

The guy next to me exclaimed, "No shit."

His friend punched his arm. "Dude, ladies present."

"Right. Sorry. Happy birthday, by the way."

Julia was still getting used to the attention from strangers. "Thanks."

He smiled at me. "First timers?"

"Yeah."

"How many times you seen it?"

"Four. Maybe five. You?"

"Gotta be dozens."

His friend laughed. "Tell the truth. He owns it. VHS, DVD, Blueray, the whole nine."

I loved movie fans. Movies had often been my salvation, carrying me through confusing and painful times, forcing me to laugh and forget daily life and giving me a safe place to cry. In L.A., I'd gone to the movies at least once or twice a week. Now I hardly ever went. Parades, festivals and free concerts filled my calendar.

The lights lowered and the theatre erupted into hooting and applause. The cartoon candy and soda danced across the screen while Mom sang along, "Let's all go to the lobby..." With her hand in the popcorn bucket and a giant smile on her face, she looked even more youthful than Julia in the flickering light. Yeah, I still loved movies.

We were deep in discussion about the characters and funny moments when we poured into the house and headed down the dark hallway. Julia seemed genuinely delighted. "Your friend is like The Dude?"

"No, my friend is The Dude and the character in the movie is sorta like him. The Coen brothers liked the whole 'holy fool' aspect of Jeff, how his steadfast existence in changing times served as a comfort." My fingers switched on the chandelier.

Mom gasped as she slammed her arm across my chest like we were heading for a car crash.

Julia laughed from behind us. "You scared me." Then she saw it too, a half dozen or so crystals standing straight out. "Whoa!"

I started toward the light and Mom put her hand over her mouth. I reached my hand out to touch one of the crystals and Julia yelled, "Don't!"

As my outstretched hand crept closer, the crystals dropped and tinkled against each other. "Weird, right?"

"Holy crap!" Julia was pale.

Mom crept closer, watching the crystals clink. She looked around the room then back to the chandelier. "Hello?"

"It doesn't talk, Mom. It's weird, not possessed."

Julia hadn't come in the room.

"Do you need to switch beds with me? I'm used to sleeping in here."

Mom reached out for Julia's hand. "Look, see? There's nothing. It's just something fascinating, not something dangerous. See?" She reached up and flicked one of the crystals with her fingernail.

Julia started laughing. "That was crazy! That was... I thought you were, I don't know, I thought you meant like it... I don't know what I thought."

"You thought I made it up."

"No, but, exaggerated maybe? I don't know what I thought."

Mom clapped her hands. "Well, I think it's time to get some sleep. Let's count your money, Julia, then wash up for bed."

I had to admit I was kinda glad the chandelier had acted up in front of them. It never hurt to have witnesses.

Chapter 12

We'd started the day walking through the sculpture garden of City Park. After wandering past a giant safety pin, a man made of letters and the colorful LOVE pop-art sculpture, I led them across a vast lawn past people paddle-boating on a pond. A breeze kicked up as we approached the Singing Oak. "This is one of my favorite places in the whole city."

Julia looked up at the sprawling live oak laden with chimes ranging from front-porch-sized to twice the height of a basketball player. "A tree?"

"I call it the 'Bing Bong Tree.' Listen."

Mom was already tuned in to the calming chaotic symphony.

"Lay down. Sometimes, if I lay here a few minutes, I can actually feel it going through me, like on a cellular level. It's pretty cool."

We all found places on the grass and spread ourselves like snow-angels. I never had to ask Mom to relax. She was always looking for opportunities. Julia and I took a little longer to give in and let go. We let the binging and bonging vibrate through us for awhile, feeling our connection to the planet, each other and the tree-music. Then we stood and shook the grass off when the ants came for us.

Lunch was barbecue shrimp. Unlike other places, our barbecue shrimp had nothing to do with barbecue sauce or grills. It was made on top of the stove with gobs of butter then served with a baguette. It was messy, but Julia liked having permission to eat with buttery fingers and sop sauce with torn bread leaving crumbs and drips all over the linen tablecloth. Dessert was bread pudding covered in a rum creme sauce that we split three ways.

Though Uptown was becoming a bit L.A. for me with its Whole Foods and pilates studio, we decided to pop into Bryan Batt's shop, Hazelnut. The display windows were filled with elegant ceramics and glassware. Enameled cuffs and beaded earrings crowded shelves along with jeweled photo frames. The whole place smelled of sweet, musky candles.

Bryan was just coming out of the back as we made our way down the aisles. "Ladies! You came!" His hair was impossibly perfect. "Perfect timing. I just got something wonderful I'm dying to show off. Come see."

We followed him to the counter near the back of the store. A young saleswoman got out of the way as Bryan ran his hands over a pile of documents. "I'm working on a new collection and sometimes I draw inspiration from old documents and drawings. I was just going through this bunch of old letters and things I recently purchased from an estate sale. I don't even know what treasures I've acquired."

Julia lifted her eyes to his. "Can I touch them?"

He cautioned. "Let's look together. I'm thinking of scanning them and using it to create a fabric or perhaps paper strips to do decoupage on furniture."

Julia smiled. "Cool!"

He separated the yellowed, brittle papers a bit and

spread them across the countertop. Fancy script divulged names, addresses and dates. "Look, a Discharge Certificate." He pulled out the paper to inspect it more closely then placed it in front of my mother before grabbing another with an elaborately printed border. "A Confederate States of America Loan. 1863. Wow."

Mom laughed. "Not worth the paper it was printed on then. Might be considerably more valuable now."

"What's this?" Julia tapped at the corner of a folded document. "Maybe we get to read someone's letter."

Bryan tugged the document out and held it up for us to see. "There's a wax seal. Maybe we can pry it open with a letter opener."

"Do you think you should? What if it's important?" A bell rung and Mom turned to smile at the postman who entered.

"You're back." Bryan was searching a cup full of pens and pencils, the folded document on the counter beside him.

A raised seal was pressed into perfectly preserved wax the color of dried blood. I leaned in to look closer.

The postman extended an envelope. "Looks like I forgot one." Something caught his eye and he retracted. "Ain't a stamp on it. How did this one..." He held it out again. "Did you mail this? Got your address both places. Return too."

Bryan took it, turned it over and back again. "Maybe Trevor or one of the others did."

Julia perked up at the mention of Trevor. It hadn't

occurred to me she might think he was cute in that way. He was far too old for her. She couldn't help herself, "Trevor works here?"

"He helps out sometimes. Between movie jobs. Should be back soon." He nodded to the postman. "Do I owe you money? For the stamp?"

"Naw, you fine." He rummaged through his sack then walked out waving. "See ya tomorrow."

Bryan opened the envelop and pulled out a photo printed on regular paper. His eyes widened. "What the... what is this?"

My voice sounded alarmed and Julia's sounded excited as we both asked, "What?"

The bell rang again and Trevor pushed the door with one hand while carrying coffees in a cardboard tray with the other. Julia smiled and adjusted her skirt.

Trevor flashed his perfect teeth. "Hey ladies. How's everyone? Y'all shopping?"

Bryan held the photo out to him. "Look."

Trevor's smile dropped as he took the piece of paper. "What the... what is this?"

"I told you someone was following me."

I suddenly felt we were invading their private space, like we were eavesdropping.

Mom was bolder. "What's it a picture of?"

Trevor handed the photo back to Bryan and he stared at it a moment before deciding to share. "It's me unlocking the door for Trevor."

I stole a glance of the slightly pixelated image over Bryan's shoulder. "Those aren't the same clothes you're wearing. Do you know when you wore this?"

Bryan looked again. "Yesterday, yes?" He showed

it to Trevor again.

Trevor nodded. "Where did you get this? Who sent it?"

Julia jumped in. "The postman just brought it. But it doesn't have a stamp."

I stared at the envelop Bryan had dropped on the counter. "No postmark either." I had Bryan's attention. "So this never went through the post office. Someone slipped it into the postman's bag? Or maybe they handed it to him with a stack of outgoing mail? No, he would have put that somewhere different, right? A different pocket or something for outgoing. And I always see them looking through outgoing mail before they put it in their bag. No, someone probably slipped it in his bag. Bryan, you said he was back. He came by earlier with another delivery?"

Bryan looked to Trevor. "Before you left. He dropped off a stack of things bound by a rubber band and a couple catalogs."

Trevor looked confused. "He came back?"

Julia was ready again. "He said he thought he'd overlooked it."

I walked to the glass front door and looked around the street. "So, someone had to put it in his bag or get it in his hands somehow within a few blocks of here, right? How long was he gone?"

Trevor finally handed one of the coffees to Bryan. "Had to be less than an hour. Was there a letter?"

Bryan absently placed the paper coffee cup on the counter. "I told you someone was watching me."

I moved the forgotten antique documents away from the coffee cup. "Like a stalker?"

Trevor blew at steam rising through the hole he'd

torn in the plastic lid. "We don't like to use that word."

Julia jumped in again. "Do you think it's that guy?"

Mom put her hand on Julia's shoulder. "Darlin'."

That was always enough to quiet me when I was speaking out of turn. Julia was bolder. "The guy from the bushes. At the movie." She connected with Trevor. "The guy you chased away. Remember?"

It was suddenly clear that Julia had taken Trevor's heroics very seriously that night. Though I was pretty sure Trevor was gay, I had to admit he was super-handsome and I could see how his stunts on and off camera were sexy. Like those wrestling shows, the athleticism was real even if the smoke-and-mirrors wasn't.

None of the adults spoke so Julia piped up again. I had to give her points for moxie. "Do you think it's him? You know, Aunt Charlotte solved a mystery. She found out someone's identity. Maybe she can help you find him."

Bryan looked at me. "You found someone?"

I felt out of my depth. "No. I found out who they were. But I never found her. I'm not... I don't have access to anything to track people. Besides, there's a saying - never attribute to malice that which you can attribute to incompetence. Or something like that." Bryan looked to the photo again and I felt the odd need to lighten things up. "I'm just saying there could be some other explanation of how the envelope got in his bag."

Julia pointed to the phone on the counter. "Why not call the police?"

All but Mom laughed. Mom gave Julia's shoulder a little squeeze.

Maybe Julia didn't know all of Mom's pipe-down signals. "What?"

Bryan tapped Trevor's arm. "How long did it take them to take your stolen car report?"

"Three days. But, I've heard worse. If it's not an emergency, forget it. Their plates are full."

"Wow." Julia looked liked she'd just figured out there was no Easter bunny. "Seriously?"

Finally Mom's calming voice asserted itself. "It's probably just a fan. They'd probably be mortified to know they scared you."

But my mind was racing. "It was taken from across the street or something. Maybe that alley beside the toy shop. Or a parked car. It's too blurry to be any closer. They didn't invade your space or anything. It's not like they took it inside the store."

Mom agreed too quickly. "Yes, they're probably shy. Not everyone is good with social interaction." She pushed Julia's shoulder a little. "We should probably get out of your hair and let you get back to your day."

Maybe we were making too much of it. "Thanks for sharing the old letters and things with us. Maybe I'll see you on another set soon."

Julia reminded the group, "Don't forget Charlotte can help."

I laughed. "I don't know about that." I lowered my head, stared at the old papers to avoid their eyes. "I'm happy to try if you want but I'm no expert on anything."

Then I spotted it. The seal pressed into the wax

on the folded document. It was the same symbol as the one on the chandelier. "Mom!" I snatched the paper up and held it for her to see. "Look. It's the symbol. The one from Dad's pipe."

She gingerly took the yellowed paper from me. "Is that it? Who remembers? I haven't seen it in decades."

"Mom, this is the symbol." I pointed to the document between her fingertips. "Bryan, where did you get this? Whose seal is this?"

"I have no idea. I bought these as a bundle at an estate sale."

"Whose estate?" I was suddenly optimistic about figuring out what the symbol was, where it'd come from.

Bryan finally opened the lid on his coffee and stirred milk and one Sweet n' Low into it. "The Broussards. But it's a collection. They don't all belong to the family. The father was a Civil War buff. He had swords, coins, all sorts of things. He passed childless, and his widow had no interest."

"Can we open it?" I hoped curiosity would be enough. I wasn't sure how to explain about the haunted chandelier, the flask at the brothel and my father's hand-carved pipe.

He took a sip of coffee and enlisted Trevor. "Can you find the letter opener? I couldn't locate it."

"It should be in the cup with the pens and pencils."

"Should be. We all seem to agree on that." This seemed like an ongoing conversation. Trevor reached into his back pocket and pulled out a Swiss Army knife. "I'll find it later. Here."

Bryan set the document down on the counter and edged the knife blade under the bubbled edge of the seal. The tip slid in easily so he twisted the blade slightly. We all gasped as the wax popped free.

My heart was banging on my ribs.

Bryan carefully unfolded the aged paper and another folded paper slipped out. He gingerly opened the paper. "It's a bill of sale." He moved the rest of the documents aside and smoothed the bill of sale onto the counter.

We all huddled around it and tried to decipher the florid script.

Julia recoiled. "It's for a person. Look."

Bryan read. "Know all men by the... something something..."

Mom offered, "Is that a name? Leonard someone? Of somewhere parish... Trustee for somebody Walls? Or Wells..."

I rushed ahead, "Have for the consideration of ninety dollars to me... something... in hand maybe? Paid by somebody Buckner? Is that a name? I think that's a name. Now recorded for the something Parish blah, blah, blah bargained and sold a certain negro woman named Lottie aged about twenty-two which slave I warrant the right and title blah, blah something about sound and healthy... Whoa. And that said negro woman Lottie is a slave for life. Witness my hand and seal this third day of January 1864. Then they signed it. Leonard Percy? Party? Purty? and Orville Buckner. They just signed her life away."

Julia looked genuinely rattled.

I couldn't take my eyes off the wax seal pressed next to Leonard's signature.

Bryan tilted the paper to let the light play on the seal. "You know what this looks like?"

I nearly yelled, "No! Please tell me."

Mom covered. "A musical instrument?'

Trevor offered, "It looks like an insect or something. A weapon maybe?"

Bryan looked again. "A pump. Doesn't it? Like an old pump?"

Once I saw it, I almost couldn't un-see it. "A pump. Like for water?"

"Yes. Trevor, hand me that book." Bryan motioned to a book full of colorful photos of Louisiana homes. He paged through, then stopped on a shot of someone's garden. An antique pump accented a decorative water feature.

"A pump." I had hoped the symbol would reveal more. Some sort of clue. A water pump didn't seem like much to go on. "Could I take a photo of the seal?" I tapped Julia who pulled out her phone.

Bryan offered up the outer paper and Julia snapped a shot. He clarified, "Why don't you borrow this. I can't think of a thing I'd need it for. I already have the seal on the bill of sale and other than that, it's just an old piece of paper."

Julia laughed. "Really old."

Bryan slipped the paper into one of his shop's bags and handed it to me.

"Really? Thanks. I'll take good care of it, I promise."

"I have no doubt."

The rest of our day was full of exploring and marvelous food but I couldn't get my mind off of the water pump. Why a pump? Was that the guy's name?

Leonard Pump? Pumpy?

The chandelier was well-behaved and since I'd taken no photos, my blog on Bryan's shop took no time at all. I posted it on Facebook then pulled the bed out of the couch and got ready for bed.

As was my habit, I checked for likes and clicks before turning in. Trevor had liked it and shared the post on his page. I sent him a "friend" request. The flexed-muscle guy had liked it as well. That was nice of him. Didn't seem his cup of tea given his limited interests. I checked his page again to see if he'd filled in any more information about himself. Perhaps he deserved a friend request as well. Nothing new and still only a few dozen friends, but Trevor and Wendy from wardrobe were among them. I checked his "likes" list. Lots of stunt things, a few locally-shot movies, Hazelnut, Bryan's public page, *Mad Men*... I was sensing a theme. Maybe this kid was the one who'd taken the photo of Bryan and Trevor.

I went back to Trevor's page and looked at his likes. A local gym, some martial artists, lots of stunt things, a few locally-shot movies, Hazelnut, Bryan's public page, *Mad Men*... Maybe Bryan was just popular with the muscle crowd. Maybe flexed-muscle guy was gay. Maybe it was an anonymous page because he wasn't out. It made sense that he'd identify with Bryan's character on *Mad Men* if he were closeted.

What if it were Trevor's page? What if he was hiding behind another identity? Was Trevor gay? Was he out? But he couldn't have taken a photo of himself opening the shop, right? Actually, the building across the street had a bunch of window sills. He could've

111

set up the camera or his phone and walked across the street, opened the store and then come back a moment later to retrieve it. He wasn't there when the postman came. He was actually gone at exactly the time he would've had to slip the envelope in the postman's bag. Wait, he said he was in the store when the postman first came. He could've slipped it in the bag then left to get coffee. It was kind of a perfect alibi. None of us suspected him. He seemed to be more of a candidate for victim than perpetrator. It was something to think about.

I closed the computer, turned off the light and thought about water pumps until I fell asleep.

Chapter 13

Mom and Julia were primping for our trip across the lake to see Aunt Ava so I decided to check my blog hits. When the browser window popped open, a headline stopped me. I turned on the TV to find images of the Deepwater Horizon oil rig engulfed in flames. Eleven men missing. "Mom!"

Mom came into the room buttoning her blouse. "Yes? My word. Where is that?"

"The Gulf. They still can't find eleven of the men."

"Awful."

"What's awful?" Julia dropped a mirror in her leather purse and clicked it shut.

Mom pointed to the TV. "Oil rig explosion."

"That's an oil pump? Won't the oil get in the water?"

"God, I hope not." Mom motioned for me to turn it off. "Off we go. We have a long drive ahead of us."

Jason, the neighbor, was just coming out of his unit as we spilled onto the landing. "Hell of a thing, yeah? The explosion? Tom must be going crazy. Didn't he have friends on that rig?"

"Oh lordy." If Mom had been wearing pearls, she would've clutched them.

I chose to be honest. "We've been in sort of radio silence mode while my mom and niece are visiting." I absently made introductions as I realized how long it had been since Tom and I had spoken.

I remained in a haze as we crossed the super-long causeway over Lake Pontchartrain. The radio kept us in the loop and Julia continued to worry about oil leaking into the water. She kept calling the rig an "oil pump" until Mom finally corrected her. "It's a drill. I don't think it was pumping anything. They have a lot of safety measures. It might be that the well sealed during the explosion."

In the rearview, I could see Julia staring out over the choppy lake. She looked unconvinced. Finally she fussed, "This sucks. Drills? Pumps? Wells? Why not just use solar? Or wind? Or water? Fossil fuels suck."

Mom's father had made his money in oil so we exchanged a glance and remained quiet. Oil had put food on our family's table but Julia wasn't wrong.

Wait! Pumps and wells. Wells. Wasn't that the name on the bill of sale? The name of whoever Leonard was the trustee for, the actual owner of the slave. Lottie. "Hey! Remember the wax stamp, the symbol? What if it didn't mean pump, what if it meant well? Like a water well."

Julia puzzled with me. "Wouldn't you just put a picture of a well? Like with a bucket and everything?"

Mom laughed. "Like a wishing well?"

I stopped them. "But what if their name was Wells? What if they used the pump to symbolize their name?"

Mom clapped. "You solved it! Another mystery solved by my amazing daughter."

"But wait, let's say I'm right. Let's say it's the

Wells plantation's symbol or something. How does their symbol end up on Sassy's chandelier, a flask at a brothel in New Orleans and Dad's pipe? I guess the flask might have been Leonard whoever's. He could have left it behind or given it to one of the women there as a gift or payment or whatever."

Julia was finally sunny again. "That makes sense."

"Charlotte loves it when things make sense." Mom knew me best. "Maybe your Aunt Ava knows something more about the chandelier. She and Sassy were pretty close when Sassy was raising her kids. And she remembers Mama Heck better than I do. That was her 'other mother' Julia." Though they were sisters, Ava was nearly a generation older than Mom so her memories reached back into the the 1930's.

We pulled up in front of the Katrina-proof house Ava had moved to after The Storm. I was always excited to see her, but now I was on a mission.

Lillibette was preparing a lunch of shrimp-salad stuffed tomatoes while Aunt Ava directed from her cushy high-back chair in the adjacent solarium. Hugs and cheek kisses were exchanged before we settled into wicker seats surrounded by ferns and African violets.

Lillibette spooned the last of the plump shrimp into an already overflowing tomato and put the bowl into the sink. "Y'all heard about the rig?"

Aunt Ava shook her head. "Lawd, Lawd. Terrible thing. Terrible. And all those missing men." She looked to Julia then changed her tone. "Let's not let it spoil your visit. Everyone send up a prayer and let's be done with it."

We were all quiet for a moment. Then Lillibette set up a tray in front of her mother and topped it with a silk placemat and a linen napkin. She handed us napkins and offered trays, which we accepted. Mom tapped Julia's seated leg, "Darlin', while you're up, could you help Lillibette with those trays?"

I was glad to finally have a younger generation to wait on me after years of being the one who might have to do something "while I was up."

I led the blessing and added a sentiment for the missing men. Lillibette was an excellent cook, and the tomatoes were perfectly ripe so lunch was distractingly delicious. As was the norm, while eating this great meal, we discussed other great lunches we'd had and other great tomato dishes.

Finally, I could no longer wait for a subtle segue. "Aunt Ava, do you know anything about Sassy's chandelier? Where she got it?"

She dabbed her rose-lipsticked lips with the cloth napkin. "Didn't she get it from Mama Heck? It was passed down."

"Yes, but where did Mama Heck get it?"

She smoothed the napkin back onto her lap. "Oh darlin', I don't think I could tell you. She just always had it. Think her Mama passed it to her."

Mom clarified, "Mama Eunoe."

"Yes."

Julia joined in. "Where'd she get it from?"

"Mama Eunoe?" She looked to Lillibette for help and found none. "Perhaps it was a family heirloom from her mother."

Mom shook her head. "No, that far back, they'd've been slaves."

Aunt Ava nodded. "You're right. As I recall, Mama Eunoe was born a slave."

Julia stopped eating. "That doesn't seem that far back. Sassy was your age, right Aunt Ava?"

"Just about, darlin'."

"You"re saying her grandmother was born a slave?"

Sometimes I had to wonder if young people understood how close we all were to separate bathrooms, segregated schools and sitting on the backs of buses. Heck, Julia had trouble believing Mom wasn't allowed to teach school when she was pregnant with me. I clarified, "Yes. She was born a slave. But she died free."

"That's crazy." Julia absently went back to her salad. "So was Maw Maw's grandmother a slave owner?"

Aunt Ava started counting back in her head then needed to say it out loud to keep it straight. "Maw Maw's Maw Maw was... It goes Mother then Ruby then Lily. For sure Lily's parents were. They had a grand plantation just north of here. Huge. Hundreds of slaves. Hundreds. Can you imagine? Lily, who is your great-great-great-grandmother, grew up with every imaginable privilege. Then the story goes that she fell in love with the overseer and her father disowned her."

I interjected. "That's my favorite part of the story." I looked at Julia. "It means we come from the woman who left all of that behind for love."

Ava laughed. "Yes, and left all that family money behind to Lawd knows who."

Lillibette laughed and brought her plate to the

sink. "Not us. That's who."

Julia looked around the lavish home. Maybe she didn't know how many times this family had started over with nothing. She was used to seeing Aunt Ava surrounded by finery. "Why did her dad disown her?"

Ava took that one. "She wanted to marry the overseer. Overseers worked in the fields with the slaves so they were seen as the same social strata as slaves."

"Seriously?"

Aunt Ava handed her plate to Lillibette then folded her napkin and placed it on her tray. "The family tree says she had a sister and two brothers. One brother died in the war fighting for the Confederacy. I suppose the other one got the plantation."

Julia finished her salad and took her dish to the sink. "What about the sister? Wouldn't she have gotten half?" She came back for the rest of our dishes. Good girl. Ava would like that.

"I think the sister may have gone with Lily. Either way, I'm not sure if they passed property to the girls back then. We aren't Creole. Creoles passed to the smartest child regardless of sex or birth order. Always seemed more civilized to me. Charlotte's favorite part is her choosing love over money, but my favorite part of the story is the chandelier. Supposedly, she took the family chandelier with her when she left."

Though I'd heard the story my whole life, this part was beginning to bother me more and more. "Don't you think it's odd that both stories have a chandelier? Seems strange all these people dragging chandeliers all over kingdom come."

Ava was totally serious. "How else would they get their chandeliers from one home to another?"

"I guess." Still, it seemed strange.

Lillibette sat down with a cocktail, handing a second to Aunt Ava. I took it as my cue to get up and help with the dishes.

Ava checked the clock on the intercom. "When does your tour start?"

Mom put all the trays away. "Two-fifteen."

Julia stacked plates in the dishwasher. "Can we see the family tree? Do you have it?"

"Oh darlin', it's in a box somewhere in the attic. Don't make Lillibette look for it. Maybe another time."

I was at least as disappointed as Julia, I was just a little better at hiding it. "Where was the plantation?"

"The Wells Plantation? I want to say St. Francisville."

I jumped. "What did you just say? Did you just say the Wells Plantation?"

"Yes, the Wells Plantation in St. Francisville. Lily Wells. Surely you know this, Charlotte. Helen, have you not taught this child our names?"

Mom looked stunned. "I showed her the tree."

Now Ava looked a little peeved. "Do you not know our names?"

Mom looked up like she was searching her brain. "Mother was born Henrietta Perry, daughter of Ruby and Oliver Perry."

Aunt Ava corrected. "Oliver Wells Perry, son of Lily Wells Perry."

I grabbed a pen and wrote the names on a pad next to the phone. "Who was the dad? Oliver's dad."

"Someone Perry I suppose. I didn't memorize every name." She shot a look at Mom. "But I certainly knew the names of our mother's mothers."

I laughed and explained to Julia, "Aunt Ava's a big believer in 'mother's baby, father's maybe.'"

Julia looked confused for a minute. Then, "Oh. Oh, that's terrible."

Ava laughed. "That's biology, sugah."

I forged ahead. "Then who was her mother?"

"Lady Wells, the mistress of the manor."

Mom laughed. "That means she doesn't remember."

Ava sassed, "Well, if I'd known there was going to be a quiz, perhaps I'd've boned up."

Mom grabbed her purse from a side bench. "You remembered a lot more than I did. A-minus to my C-plus."

My mind was spinning. "Julia, do you have that photo you took of the wax seal? Show Ava."

Julia retrieved her phone and scrolled through it. She tapped the screen then showed it to Ava.

Ava held the phone to the light. "You know I'm all but blind. What am I looking at?"

I wished I was still young enough to believe in crossing my fingers. "It's a wax seal with a symbol stamped into it. We think it might be a symbol for a water well, an old-fashioned pump. Can you see it?"

She held the phone further away, then closer. "Hand me my magnifying glass, Lillibette."

Lillibette got up and brought her the beautifully silver-framed glass. Ava studied the image as Lillibette looked over her shoulder.

"Do you recognize it?"

She handed me the phone. "No, but my eyes aren't what they used to be. Do you know it, Bette?"

"No. What's it from?"

I tried to remain optimistic. "On a bill of sale. It was from the trustee of a plantation selling a slave to someone in New Orleans. It was hard to read but the name could have been Wells. I was thinking maybe the symbol was for a well."

"I could see that," Lillibette offered.

"Wouldn't that be something? I suppose it could be from our family plantation."

"The symbol was on the chandelier too. Sassy's chandelier."

"Huh. Well, that really would be something."

Julia added, "And Paw Paw's pipe."

Ava laughed. "Your Paw Paw? As in Charlotte's father? I don't think so. He married in."

She shrugged. "Weird, right?"

Ava stood to see us out. "It sounds like maybe our family farm sold its fair share of goods back in the day. I'm telling you, the place was very large and prosperous before the war. You know, the Yankees came and took a lot of that stuff after the war, sold it off. There's probably Wells' family heirlooms all over the state."

I hugged her shrinking frame. "I suppose. That does make sense. But what are the odds of Sassy having a Wells chandelier in the same house as the Wells family descendants? It has to be the same chandelier, right? Doesn't that make more sense than there being two chandeliers that left that plantation? One with a runaway daughter and the other with a slave's daughter? It's the same chandelier, right?"

She brushed a curl from my cheek. "You always did love puzzles."

Mom and I had done this drive many times. We had let Julia choose the plantation. We presented her with Oak Alley, best known for its tree-lined walkway of 300 year old sprawling live oaks that had been planted long before the farm was built. It remained a mystery who'd originally seeded the twenty-eight trees leading from the river to the empty field that would eventually become a monumental manor home. Then we tempted Julia with Laura Plantation, the only preserved Creole plantation. She liked the idea of learning about Creole culture, especially since it was a more merit-based society and the farm was named for the woman who last ran it.

But the winner was Evergreen, a farm Mom and I hadn't yet toured. Driving up, the grand white manor home imposed itself on a large lawn. Swooping staircases bowed out on either side of the landing's massive columns, like dimples on a majestic facade.

Having just imagined our own family's plantation, Mom and I were more curious than usual. For Julia, everything was new. Renee, the tour guide, gathered us in the parking lot and led us across the lawn to take in the front of the house explaining that the home had been built in 1790 on 2200 acres. The privately owned sugar farm was still functioning, which I found amazing and a little romantic. As a child of divorce, I was always looking for through-lines and continuity.

Renee talked about when the French Creole farmhouse was redone in the Greek Revival mode in

1832 and the symmetrical staircases were added. The house was smaller inside than Julia expected. She was also shocked by how short the beds were.

Outside, our group toured the grounds behind the house which was bookended with garconnieres and pigeonniers on either side of the home. Renee explained that garconnieres were bachelor pads for the adult sons and pigeonniers were giant bird houses to harvest eggs and fowl for food and dung for fertilizer. The garden behind the house was symmetrically maze-like and manicured. Since the farm had never been abandoned, everything was in amazing shape. It was easy to picture women preparing a meal in the kitchen, someone collecting eggs, even someone ducking into the outhouse and dealing with a hoop skirt.

Like Oak Alley, the property had a gorgeous lane of eighty-two live oaks. At first look down the alley dripping with Spanish moss, I half expected to see a mansion standing proudly at the end. Instead, behind the trees on both sides of the lane stood twenty-two one-room Cyprus duplex shacks meant to hold two entire families each.

Documents regarding the property were on display, including an inventory of possessions. Whatever visions I may have had of children playing in the lane or people sitting on their porches came down to this - "West, 36, Mulatto, excellent blacksmith and engineer and good subject, estimated $1500. Joe, Congo field hand, $300. Eblany, 21, American negress field hand with her two children, $1000."

It was difficult to reconcile the complicated

history of mammies and clandestine lovers and children playing together until they were told that one was "to the manor born" and the other was property. I could see Julia was trying to make it all make sense.

Mom stared at the inventory. "Can you imagine being in your own home and having invaders drag you off in chains to endure a months-long trip in a boat only to be sold upon arrival in your new country? Imagine not knowing the language, not practicing the same faith, being stripped of all of your possessions and then finding yourself farming at the end of someone's whip." She shook her head. "Hard to believe we came from all of this."

I sighed. "That's why I always loved the story of Lily. It comforts me to know we're descended from the person who left all that behind for love."

"Amen." She shook it off and shot Julia a smile. "This was a good choice, Julia. This place has it all - the good, the bad and the ugly."

Renee agreed. "The estate is known as the most intact plantation complex in the south." That seemed to impress many in the tour group.

I was always curious about people's daily lives. "How did you come to work here? Are you a history buff?"

"It's funny you ask. Somethin' drew me to this place."

"Really? That's kinda cool. Like a vibe?"

She pushed her sandy-blonde hair behind her ear. "I was just drawn to it. I'd already been working at the estate for a couple of years when I found out that my eleven-generations-ago grandfather had designed the home."

"Are you serious? That's awesome!" Sometimes I could hear how L.A. I sounded.

Julia was far more articulate and mature. "That's incredible. You must've felt like a big question was answered."

Renee thought about that. "Yes. It was like somethin' here had been speakin' to me and finally I could make sense of it."

"We're looking into a family story." Mom was forever telling people personal things about her day. "Show her the seal, Charlotte."

I motioned to Julia who pulled out her phone and found the image. Renee took the phone and stared. "It's a pump?"

I laughed. "Where were you months ago? Thing's been bugging me for months. We just figured out the pump thing yesterday. Would you think this could be the symbol for a well?"

"Oh sure."

It was worth a shot, "Have you heard of a Wells Plantation? Could be from there, couldn't it?"

She shook her blonde waves. "No, can't recall a Wells Plantation. Here on the River Road?"

"No. Saint Francisville."

"Myrtles and Rosedown are the only ones I know 'round there. But I haven't studied the area much. But it does stand to reason that a Wells Plantation would use that for a seal."

Julia kept her eyes on the shacks. "Does that mean they would brand the slaves with it?"

"It might. That's the thing about southern stories, there can be a lot of ugly in our beauty."

I added, "Over and over, what didn't kill this

region seems to have made it stronger. Right now, the state of Louisiana is the most politically diversified state in the United States. Did you know that? We have the nation's first Indian governor, Bobby Jindal, black mayors including Cedric B. Glover, Shreveport's first black mayor, and our mayor - Nagin. We also have the first Vietnamese American congressman, Joseph Cao, and a female senator, Mary Landrieu."

Mom, Renee and several of the other tour-takers had obviously not seen our state as a leader of diversity until that moment. Julia was less impressed, this being her third year with a black President.

Renee smiled. "I feel like I learned somethin' new today. Certainly, I knew all of that. Heck, I voted for some of those folks. But, I never did put it together that way."

We talked about the plantation the whole way back into the city. We kept talking about it as we dressed for a red carpet, Mom and Julia in the gowns they'd worn when we worked on the movie. And we kept on talking about it until the valet came to take our car under the signature aqua-and-white awning of Commander's Palace. Friendly faces offered, "Welcome in" as we followed the warm hostess through the main dining room with the birds coming out from the wallpaper, up the stairs, through smaller rooms and into the glass-walled garden room overlooking a courtyard with massive trees covered in twinkle lights. Our table next to the window was one of several festooned with birthday balloons.

We ordered the Soup 1-1-1 so Julia could try their Gumbo, Turtle Soup and Soup du Jour - a crawfish bisque. We also ordered a broad variety of entrees for maximum tasting. I tried to describe "ballet service" to Julia but she couldn't picture it until the wait staff surrounded the table and lowered their dishes in front of us simultaneously, liked they'd been elegantly choreographed.

All of the food was amazing but the Strawberry Shortcake made from a buttermilk biscuit topped with fresh Ponchatoula strawberries and Chantilly crème was outstanding. We all sang to Julia as she blew out her candle wearing the tall paper chef hat all birthday-celebrators were awarded.

I wrote our waitresses' name down and asked her for our table number. Michelle was a second generation server at Commander's and proud of it. I loved that. After she left us in full food-induced afterglow, Julia whispered to me, "Why did you get the table number and stuff?"

"I'm going to ask for her and this table next time I come. This was a perfect night, right?"

She had to agree. "An A-plus."

"Well, this is the kind of place where perfect is repeatable. Now I have a favorite table and a favorite waitress."

Mom stood and gathered her purse. "Will Tom be able to join us at the movie?"

"I don't think so, but I'll check my phone when we get outside."

We wound our way down the back steps and through the organized hustle the kitchen before landing back at the hosting room to say our goodnights. I handed the ticket to the valet and pulled out my flip phone. The text read, "Sorry Slim. Still waiting to hear about friends. Can't focus. Terrible company. Have fun." I wanted to be angry at him. I at least wanted to feel entitled to my disappointment. But I couldn't imagine spending the day watching a rig burn in the middle of the Gulf and my friends nowhere to be seen since the explosion. "He can't come."

Mom hated it when men didn't show up for me. We both did. She smiled. "What a wonderful supper. Now we get to have an glamorous night at the movies with Carter." Mom loved Carter. She didn't want me to date him - she called him a "rascal" because he had a more-is-more approach to women, but she loved him all the same.

We were running late but there were a few photographers remaining at the carpet so I excused myself and walked the line. Mom and Julia waited by the box office. I could hear Mom saying how amazing it was to be at The Prytania for a premiere after coming here as a kid on a scooter. I almost never posed with anyone on the carpet. Pose with a movie star and you're marked for life. Pose with someone random and it reduces the value of the photo. But I suddenly didn't care about what was smart or strategic. I leaned across the rope and looked in one of the photographers' eyes. "That's my mother and my niece. We're celebrating her birthday. Can they come on the carpet with me?"

As they joined me on either side, I noticed most of the photographers worked for local papers and magazines. One was using her phone as a camera. They probably weren't looking for a shot to sell on WireImage. "Mom was a regular here as a child, right

Mom?"

Mom ran with it, giving her story and name to a couple of the reporters. She mentioned our meal and Julia's hat that we'd left in the car then told them about us working together on a movie. I liked that they got to be the "stars" for a moment.

Carter was coming out of the restroom as we grabbed popcorns and Cokes. His face lit up when he spotted me. "Charlotte!" He gave me a big, long hug then pushed me to arm's length to get a better look. "You look amazing, as usual. Love the shoes." Then he turned to Mom and hugged her. "Helen."

"Carter, this is my granddaughter, Julia."

He smiled at her and took her hand. "Are you a hugger?"

"Sure."

They shared a short embrace then he put his arm around my waist and grabbed my popcorn from the counter. "Come on. I'll show you where we're sitting."

Other than Carter, I had no connection to *Contenders* so I'd expected to have to find three unassigned seats together. But Carter led us to a reserved row and settled in next to me. Julia hit my hand and nodded her head to some of the other stars sitting nearby. I liked seeing this through her eyes - her expression reminded me that this was rare air and not just part of the job.

Carter leaned into my neck. "I'm so glad you came. The kids couldn't come and you know I hate doing this stuff alone."

The kids were so grown now, I hardly knew what to ask about them anymore. "How are they?"

"They're great. Amazing. Suzy just won an award at her school. They had a whole presentation. I was that ridiculously proud parent annoying everyone with my cell phone filming the whole thing."

I laughed. "More 'Carter Ellis is a nerdy jerk' stories."

I loved it when I could get him to laugh. His eyes would crinkle and the lines looked like the trails of shooting stars. He called them "crows feet" and hated them. Getting old as a heartthrob in Hollywood was no picnic, even for men.

Mom sang along to the animated dancing soda and candy, "Let's all go to the lobby, to get ourselves a treat!" I wished I could please myself with the same abandon she did. I was doing my best just to resist shushing her.

Carter laughed. "You tell 'em, Helen!"

Sometimes I had to remind myself not to fall in love with him.

The opening credits began and everyone clapped for the producers, the title, each of the stars and on and on. Carter was the clear crowd favorite.

The movie was pretty good, a solid sequel. Carter was great. I was glad I didn't have to worry about Tom hating it.

We went to the ladies room as people crowded around Carter and a line formed to shower him with praise.

As we joined the bathroom line, Julia looked at me with new eyes, like she'd just solved a puzzle in me. "Is there always so much clapping?"

"You mean at the end? Pretty much but you can tell when they really like the movie."

"I mean from the beginning."

I snorted a laugh. "Yeah, usually. I mean, the people are usually sitting right there so it's kind of like applauding at a play where they can actually hear your applause."

"Before you see the movie? Doesn't it make more sense to applaud just the ending credits?"

I hadn't ever thought of it that way. "You know, it took almost eight years of my life to produce that movie with Clarence. And I had <u>the</u> Clarence Poole on my side from day one. It was his idea to make the dang thing and it still took eight years. So, yeah, applaud the producers just for getting the movie made. Applaud the actors for researching, working out, learning accents and fight choreography, whatever, for giving birth to an entire human being and for daring to be judged for their work. Applaud the director, cinematographer and editor for coming up with shots, a tone, a look for the piece, a way of storytelling. Applaud the costume designer for researching, shopping, sizing, designing and sometimes sewing. It takes a village and our villages kill themselves even to make a terrible movie."

"Wow."

"Yeah. Those people you worked with the other day can work sometimes twenty-hour days. They can go months without seeing their families. Obviously, it's nothing like the military, but it takes that kind of stamina and tenacity. And faith. You're part of making something you have very little control over, working your butt off knowing it could suck and that anyone in the world can see it."

She was almost to the front of the line. "What's

your dream role? Like if you could play anything."

"Easy, Scarlett."

Mom clapped. "Oh yes. Oh she's terrible. 'If I have to lie, cheat, steal, kill, as God is my witness, I'll never go hungry again.'"

"Then after the intermission, she lies, cheats, steals and kills. Please tell me your father has taken you to see *Gone with the Wind* on the big screen."

Julia looked guilty. "Not yet."

Mom covered her mouth. I jabbered. "If you've only seen it on the TV, it comes off like a Mexican soap opera. You have to see it on the big screen first, then you can reduce it like that. The filmmakers couldn't even've pictured a world with TV's and commercials. It would kill them to know that's how most people see it. It's killin' me to know that's the only way you've seen it and I have nothing to do with making that movie."

Mom hiccuped. "Talk about faith. They filmed the burning of Atlanta before they'd even cast their Scarlett." She had loud, funny-sounding hiccups. "Oh lordy. Somebody scare me."

"So, why do you want to play Scarlett?"

"It's the greatest antihero role ever written for a woman. They don't write many so it's not a tough contest. It's the epic tale of a feisty teenager who alpha-female's her way through a very patriarchal society and dominates without ever losing her femininity. And yes, she's fabulously terrible. The ultimate diva. Like most great antiheroes, I'd never want to be her, but it might be nice to be more like her. I'd sure as heck love to play her. Although, not really. Vivien Leigh stuck a fork in that one. She's beyond perfect. I have nothing new to offer."

Mom stopped holding her breath. "As much as I'd love to see you in a hoop skirt, you're right. I love you to the moon but I don't want to see any more attempts at a remake. It's just wrong. Oh! I think I got rid of my hiccups."

But she hadn't. She was still hiccuping when we came out and found Carter standing in the lobby with the last of his hand-shakers.

"Ladies! I was afraid I lost you. I was hoping to get a coffee or something but we have to be back to the airport. Let me walk you out."

His arm looped around my waist again. It was kind of comforting being around someone from the life I left behind, someone who knew me in that world. Everywhere else I'd ever lived, I felt like a weirdo, like no one else cared about what I cared about. L.A. was no different. New Orleans was the only place where it seemed like I was surrounded by people who valued my values. But I had to admit that my career made me stand out a bit here. I was just relearning how to have normal conversations that didn't center around, "Who's your agent?" or "What are you working on?" - all of which felt like different ways of saying, "Are you useful to me?" Carter made me feel like our job was normal in that abnormal world. Plus, he had a gift for making me glow inside like a prom queen reunited with her quarterback sweetheart from back in the day. We'd never really dated, but mostly because we liked each other too much to do damage like that.

We stopped in front of his limo and he smiled his shooting-star-eyes smile. "Tell me you're happy."

I smiled back. "Happier than I've ever been. Seriously. I'm where I'm supposed to be and, so far, I've been working and getting to do what I'm supposed to be doing."

He gave me a small peck. "You'd tell me if you needed anything, wouldn't you?"

I looked down at his crisp, white collar.

"No, you never do. You just get through."

I looked into his eyes once more. "Yeah, but I don't have much to get through anymore. It's really easy for me to be happy here."

"So, you're really not coming back?"

I laughed. "Of course not. Dang Carter, I barely survived that place."

"Okay, okay." He took his arm from my waist and hugged Mom's neck.

She hiccuped in his ear. "Oh my!"

We all laughed.

He hugged Julia. "It was wonderful meeting you. Happy birthday. Yet another wonderful apple from this tree."

We blew kisses as we left then found our car down the street. Julia put her tall, paper hat on her lap. "Well, that was amazing."

I shot her a smile in the rearview. "Yay."

Chapter 14

We only had half a day left so we headed back to the French Quarter for lunch at Susan Spicer's Bayona. I'd eaten there before and found it outstanding. After we were seated, I explained that there was a character on *Treme* that was based on the James Beard Award-winning chef-owner and her struggle after Katrina. I was so glad Bayona wasn't on the list of things that "ain't der no mo'."

I made Mom and Julia order their own rustic and savory Cream of Garlic Soup. "It's way too good to split one three ways."

Mom loved her Caesar Style Salad with Lemon Pickle and Fried Capers, said it was the best salad she'd ever had. I let everyone taste my delectable Pork Cutlet with Brussels Sprouts, Cider Sauce and Potato-Parsnip Purée.

Julia adventurously tried the Smoked Duck "PB & J" of Cashew Butter, Pepper Jelly, Apple-Celery Salad and Wild Flour Multigrain. "Why is all of this so good?"

"Isn't it amazing? There's such a purity of flavor. There's all these sophisticated sauces with each dish, but they enhance the flavors instead of masking them. It's like skillfully applied make-up on a woman's face."

Mom stole a forkful of purée from my plate. "I

think it's the ingredients. I remember when food used to taste like this."

I laughed. "You mean last night? Those Ponchatoula strawberries were insane."

Mom nodded while she swallowed. "I still miss going to the festival every year."

I resisted licking my plate. "So, what was your favorite thing, Julia."

"Of the whole trip?"

Mom stole some of Julia's duck. "Oh yes, it's your first trip as a grown person. What did you love?"

Julia stopped eating for a minute. "Actually, it's easy. The drummers at the school."

Mom exclaimed, "Oh yes. Definitely."

"The Roots of Music?" I clarified.

"Yeah, them. That was the best part. Meeting Derrick and seeing the classes and everything, but especially the drummers."

Mom corrected. "Mr. Derrick."

Julia corrected her correction. "No, Derrick is his first name."

"Yes, sugah, but he's your elder."

Julia looked puzzled.

Mom shook her head. "I feel like I failed your father."

"Do I have bad manners?"

Mom and I exchanged looks. She took the lead. "No, darlin'. You're wonderful. There may be some children here who have different training than you do, but I don't think anyone could call you bad-mannered."

I tried to be supportive, "I don't say sir or ma'am that often."

Mom winked. "Well darlin, it's never too late to start."

I laughed. "Yes ma'am."

We finished our meal, thanked the staff and headed to Jackson Square. Interesting local titles filled the window of a book shop. Inside, we realized it was the gift shop of the historic 1850 House. At three dollars, two for Mom, we couldn't resist taking the tour. A couple from Ohio and a small family from Texas joined us in front of a wall of photos.

Mary, the round-faced tour guide with a hairdo from the 70's suburbs, pointed to the photo array. "Photographs were uncommon so it was very rare for anyone to photograph slaves. We're very lucky to have these."

Julia stared at a black and white portrait labeled, "Rebecca." A fair-haired, pale-skinned teenager stared vacantly. Rebecca looked a lot like Julia. "This girl is a slave?"

"Yes, she worked in the home."

Julia kept staring. "She looks... like me."

"Slaves came in many shades. Could be octoroon."

"Octoroon?"

I knew this one. "One-eighth."

Mary smiled. "Yes. One drop of slavery's blood was enough back then. Follow me. Careful on the steps."

Julia lagged behind, staring at the photo a moment longer. I wanted to tell her that people were no longer for sale, that we didn't decide people's fates anymore based on their bloodlines, that the prejudices that led us to allow slavery in a free country were a thing of the past. But I wasn't willing to lie. Life wasn't fair in ways Julia was only beginning to understand, complicated in ways she was only beginning to see. Even slavery wasn't as simple as black and white.

Mary explained the apartment was built in 1850 by the Baroness Micaela Almonester de Pontalba and illustrated middle class life in the pre-Civil War era. "These are believed to be the oldest apartment houses in the United States."

Since New Orleans had been around before America, many things here were the oldest or the first. Though they weren't the original furnishings, the house had been painstakingly recreated with pieces from the era. A beautiful glass-encased floral wall hanging made of human hair was an oddball highlight.

We finished our visit over a plate of beignets at Café du Monde. Mom licked her powdery fingers. "So, no Tom. I was hoping to meet him. Did they find his friends?"

Tom hadn't texted but I'd seen the news. All eleven were presumed dead. The still-burning rig had exploded again that morning and sunk into the Gulf. There were already reports of an oil slick in the area. "I think Tom's having a bad day."

Mom put her hand on mine. "Horrendous. And terrible timing for meeting family."

"Yeah. I mean, yes, of course, but I'm not sure he was into the whole premiere idea anyway. Maybe he was just freaked out by meeting family or by Carter. Who knows. I've had guys dump me for less. Honestly, I've never had a guy make it through me getting an acting job."

Julia looked shocked. "But you only worked one day."

"That's done me in before."

Mom smiled gently. "Sugah, that was when you were dating industry people. Tom's a regular guy with a regular job. He can't possibly be jealous of you getting work."

Julia was full-on baffled. "Why would a guy be jealous of you getting a job. It's not like they would've gotten the part if you didn't."

I pounded the table and spoons clanked against coffee saucers. "Sorry. That was more dramatic than I meant. But yes, Julia, that's what I always thought."

"Cheer up darlin'. He's probably just mourning his friends."

I laughed. "Boy, talk about a tin-foil lining. But, I'll take it."

Julia gave us some side-eye. "You guys are terrible."

I always hated the part where we had to say goodbye. I knew it would be awhile before I'd see Julia again, that she'd keep becoming more womanly, more grown. And it always wrecked me to say goodbye to my mother. We talked all the time but there was something so nurturing about actually being around her. She could irritate me but it was almost always because I was more cynical than she was. Her sunny disposition could feel relentless, but I not-so-secretly wished I were more like her.

When we parted, I always felt like the best of me was being pulled to a distance. I would leave New Orleans and cry throughout takeoff, often well into waiting for the seatbelt light to turn off. Then Mom moved to Florida (because Louisiana was too cold) and I moved to New Orleans so now, she was the one leaving home. I had to admit it, part of my crying was always over leaving the city. I still hated saying goodbye to Mom. I still cried. But as the glass doors opened and the local balmy air hit my face, I felt like I was surrounded by "the best of me." Increasingly, I was realizing New Orleans was my soul mate.

I was glowing with that feeling as I pulled up in front of our family home, built for my ancestors. I turned off the radio and hated the silence. I knew the house would feel empty when I walked in. I grabbed my bag and made my way down the overgrown path leading to the side door. The motion-detector light flashed on, flooding the leaves with light.

I saw the hoodie before I heard the rustling and jumped instinctually. "What the..."

His eyes were light brown, hazel maybe. He was about my height, five-foot-ten. Grey hoodie. Then he was gone.

My heart pounded. I called the Garden District Police as I scrambled to close the door behind me. The officer said someone would drive by and check it out. I watched from the window upstairs until I saw the SUV pull up. Officer Signal met me at the gate. "You the one called?"

"Yes, thank you. Come in." I held the gate so it wouldn't slam behind him, then led him through the overgrowth. I pointed to the fence behind the trees. "He was there, looking through the leaves. Now, for all I know, he was visiting the neighbors and came out of their back door for some reason. Maybe he was working in their yard out back. But, they have no grass. Trimming trees? Except it's dark. Shoulda been gone by now, right? But he could be a friend or something. Maybe he just freaked out and ran because the light and me being there startled him. Maybe it's like snakes, like he's more scared of me."

Officer Signal chuckled. "Maybe." He looked around, pointed his flashlight through the trees, went back out to the sidewalk and looked at the fence line. "Their gate was open when you got here?"

I suddenly realized what an asset a nosy neighbor could be. I even felt a little guilty that I hadn't paid more attention to whether someone was breaking into my neighbor's house. "I think so. I think. But, I don't really know."

"And he headed that way?" He pointed down the tree-lined street in the direction I had reported.

"Yes, about five minutes ago."

Another police SUV slowly rolled past. "Must not've found anything yet. We'll keep an eye out. Call again you see anything."

"Thanks. I will." Inside, I checked the locks twice. I'd recorded a new show being shot locally and hoped it would relax me.

I noticed every creak of the house settling, every branch scraping a screened window when a breeze gusted. Was someone trying to break into the neighbors' house? Could they get in here? How secure was this house against intrusion? What if he came up the back staircase? He'd been in the neighbors' side yard. Maybe he was scoping their backyard. Maybe he was checking ours - comparing which would be easier to breach. Or maybe he was a cousin looking for the hide-a-key.

Shocked from my winding thoughts, I jumped in my seat. "Albert!" I rewound the scene. It really was Albert. He rocked on a porch across from another weathered man. The scene was funny, and Albert was actually great - a natural. He even made me laugh twice. I never knew how to feel when a novice made my job look easy, but I couldn't wait to see Albert again and tell him he was the best thing in the show.

Chapter 15

It was unseasonably warm and sticky so I decided to splurge on some ice cream while I was at the grocery. Locals call shopping "making groceries," but I would feel as inauthentic as if I used words like "bomb" or "word" when I thought something was cool. The line was longer than usual so I stared at candy wrappers and tawdry magazine covers. Then the cashier ended her shift and had to switch out her drawer with the next cashier who then had to do some receipt-readout thing before taking a breath and scanning my goods. The ice cream was sweaty and stuck to the plastic baggie. Dang. I had a mile walk in the heat ahead of me. I felt like returning the ice cream but just wanted to leave at that point.

Heat radiated from the blacktop parking lot. I put my earbuds in and tried to shake off my irritation. In L.A., there were irritable people all over the place but here it stood out as a party foul. Still, I couldn't help but hope I didn't run into Albert and further melt my sweet treat.

When I first spotted him standing in front of Design Within Reach, it occurred to me that I could just keep walking. He was chatting with someone and hadn't spotted me so I would almost be behaving politely by not interrupting his conversation. But I had a few rules I lived by, rules that had guided me away from regret most of my life. One was - never die with your mouth full of all the nice things you meant to say. So I waved. He waved back. Dang, shoulda returned the ice cream. I thought of crossing but yelled across the street instead. "Hey Albert. I saw your show! You were great."

He and his friend smiled. "You saw?"

"Yeah, you were the best thing on it! Seriously, I mean that."

"You so sweet."

I laughed. "No, I woulda pretended I didn't see it if I didn't like it. Woulda never brought it up."

They laughed. Albert waved. "You have a blessed day."

"You too."

The ice cream was nearly soup so I threw it in the freezer and set a timer for twenty minutes. I hoped to relax but the Coast Guard guy on the TV was saying that oil was leaking at about 8,000 barrels a day. I opened my laptop and Googled. 8,000 barrels equals... 340,000 gallons. Whoa. The phone rang and I paused the news.

"Hey Slim. Where y'at?" Tom's voice was comforting.

"Just got home from the grocery. I just saw about the spill. You okay?"

"No. You free for dinner?

My heart leapt a little. I had to admit, I'd been wondering if we were okay. Maybe meeting family was too fast for him but everything else was fine. "Sure. Where ya takin' me?"

"Can we meet there? I'm kinda on call. Things are crazy right now."

"So you might have to leave." My heart sank.

"Yes."

It seemed off somehow, but there was a giant oil spill and his friends were presumed dead so it would be normal to be off. "Okay."

"Bacchanal. I'll meet you there at five-thirty. There's a good band and a friend of mine is cooking. You'll like it."

Maybe everything was fine. "Great. See you there."

"Wear bug spray."

"Oh. Okay."

I was still digging through bottles under the sink to find bug spray when the phone rang again. Marilyn. "Hey."

"Hey! Is this a good time?"

She'd never asked that before. I closed the cabinet and sat on the toilet lid. "Sure."

"How are you?"

"I'm good. What's going on?"

"I've thought about this a lot. You know I have a limited client list and two of my clients moved away this year, one got pregnant, one quit, two never work and one retired."

I didn't like where this was going.

"I've been thinking it might be time for me to retire too. Leave on a high instead of watching it all fade away."

Even though Claudia was an amazing agent, I'd been spoiled having a manager with so few clients to please. She wasn't even my manager anymore, she was my friend from work. We used to eat lunch together at least once a month. We'd chat on the

145

phone for hours about guys, the industry and people we knew. But, I was one of those clients who'd moved away. "You're retiring? Are you going to do something else?"

"I don't know. I've thought about it a lot the past couple of years but I don't really know what else I'm passionate about. I've been doing this for decades. It's really all I know."

I had that heavy-chested feeling of something ending and change coming. "Well, you were amazing at it. We were your passion and that's pretty cool. I'm going to miss it."

Marilyn breathed slowly. "I've just been doing this so long. I think I'd just like to relax for a little while."

I laughed. "It's kinda hard for me to imagine you doing nothing. You're my pit bull who never took no for an answer. And you were willing to go pretty far to chase down work." We both laughed. I took a breath. "Thank you, Marilyn. I owe you a lot and I know that. You took me from a struggling actor to a working actor and kept it all going even though I was in my thirties when we met. Thank you for believing in me."

"You deserved it. And Claudia seems great. My kinda broad. You'll be fine."

"She really is like you in a lot of ways. It's almost weird, like lightning striking twice or having two soul mates. Except I haven't met her."

"Still? How is that possible? Not even when you signed with her?"

"We don't have any paperwork."

Marilyn was silent for awhile. Then, "You know

146

what I'm going to say."

"Yes, but you're retired and I have a date to get ready for. We'll talk more later, okay?"

"Good. Okay. Talk to you later."

Bacchanal was at the end of a road lined by the old Navy yard. Across the street, Tom was waiting in front of a rustic, brick, corner building. He gave me a hug and a peck and held the door for me. I loved that.

He chose a wine and a block of cheese from a cooler in the front lobby then led me down a hall and out the back of the building. The fenced tree-shaded yard twinkled with tiny white lights. People sat in plastic lawn chairs around metal-mesh tables or industrial-sized upended spools. Cats wandered around.

Tom led me to a tent covering a makeshift kitchen. The pretty woman cooking inside wiped her hands on her batique apron and offered one to shake. "Hey, you must be Charlotte."

That was a good sign. "Hi. Your food smells great."

"Try the fish. It's super-fresh."

She leaned over the counter and hugged Tom. "Get the fish. You'll thank me."

We decided to order the fish and try the Crawfish Madeline as well. The ground beneath my chair was lumpy and I tried to find a perfect balance.

"It's pretty, right?"

It was.

He looked suddenly serious. "So, it looks like things are gettin' kind of bad for me right now. My dad's health is gettin' even worse. My mother is losin' her mind and wants me around all the time. And I have memorials to attend. Four of them. And now there's this spill. We don't know how bad that could get, but the healthy amount of oil for a wetland is zero. It's not going to be zero."

I didn't like where this was going. "Sounds like you need a little time to sort some things out."

He smiled a little. "Yeah. I thought about that. I did. But I think it's too early for all that for us. I'm a 'good time guy,' and right now, I'm not a good time."

I jumped as a cat rubbed against my calf and purred. I gathered myself. "This too shall pass. I'm fine with hanging back until things settle down for you. You know, the other thing is, I am your girlfriend so you could actually let me be there for you. You know, go through this with you."

Someone brought our food and took the number-flag from our table. I blessed my delicious-smelling meal and hoped this wasn't our last supper.

"I'm not... I'm the guy you see the city with, dance at concerts, hang out with friends, that sort of thing. My life is about to get hard and sad and I don't want to do that with you. It's too early for us. Trust me on this. You don't want to stick around for this part."

I had plenty of arguments ready but I stayed quiet.

"Charlotte, I'm a dime a dozen here. You'll find out."

After decades of hearing men blow their own horns, this was a whole new kind of approach. Maybe it was the local version of, "It's not you, it's me."

He smiled at me.

"What are you talking about? You're not a dime a dozen. I love being around you. You're great. You

148

made me a mix-tape once. I felt like a college kid again."

"You're just gonna have to trust me on this. Around here, I'm nothing special. You'll see. You'll figure it out."

It was beginning to sound like an excuse. Like he thought I would leave him so he was bailing first. "So I should be thanking you?"

He laughed. "Maybe so. But don't, I'm kinda raw right now." He took my hand. "I really loved being with you. I had thoughts I hadn't had before. This isn't easy for me, I just know I'm right. I don't want you to see me go through all this. And you shouldn't, you know? You don't owe me that. I'm not going to be myself."

I pulled my hand away. "My manager retired."

"Marilyn?"

I don't know why I wanted him to know this was bad timing for me. "Today. While I was getting ready to come here for our date. That's it."

"Sounds like we both have a lot to process."

How could he not be special when he said mature level-headed things like that? I was used to being the reasonable one. "So, that's that?"

"It's a small city. I'm sure we'll run into each other, but yeah."

Another cat rubbed against me then licked my ankle. "Well. Then I want to say that you were a great boyfriend."

He laughed. "No I'm not. My friends all gave me a hard time for not making plans every weekend, not calling you enough, not bringing you flowers or whatever. They were singing the Beyonce song about if you like it, shoulda put a ring on it. They think I'm an idiot."

His friends told him to treat me better? In L.A., guys were forever giving horrible advice about playing the field, not calling too soon, "negging" and the "third-date rule." "Okay, I'll admit it wasn't awesome sitting at home on a Friday when I had a boyfriend, but I had a great time with you."

"Then my mission is complete."

The house seemed so quiet and empty when I got home. I waited for the familiar pain of loss to wash over me. The phone rang. Sofia. "Oh, thank goodness you're calling. I'm having a day."

"Oh, okay. What happened?"

I told her about Tom saying he was a dime-a-dozen and about Marilyn retiring.

"What was that thing you used to say, sometimes God remodels your life, sometimes He knocks it down and rebuilds it?"

"Wrecking ball. I say he runs a wrecking ball through your life. You know what though? Claudia is a lot like Marilyn. It kinda freaks me out how similar they are. As people and as people who represent my career. I actually can't even believe how lucky I am to have found Claudia. It's like finding a second unicorn."

"This is a terrible pity party."

We laughed.

Sofia clattered pans in her sink. "Maybe Tom's right and this is all for the best. What if he just did you the biggest favor ever? Who wants to be around a drinker going through a bunch of tragedies? Forget about that. What did he say? You don't deserve all that? You don't. Seriously, Charlotte, run. You always say if someone tells you who they are---"

"Believe them. Yeah. I guess."

"I think you should be happy."

I laughed, "Sure, I'll throw a party. Yay, I'm alone again."

"You said you never feel alone there. You said people are always including you and that you can go to things alone there."

"Yeah."

"So, you're fine."

It wasn't a question, it was a command.

I thought about the Wednesday free concerts I'd attended alone and about the couples, longtime-friends and families that invited me to join them during Mardi Gras and the Super Bowl celebrations. "Yeah. Okay. I'm good." And I was.

It wasn't until after we hung up that it occurred to me that Sofia might've phoned because she needed something. Being self-centered seemed normal in L.A. There, I was considered pretty great girlfriend material, but maybe I was a dime-a-dozen girlfriend around here. Maybe I wasn't the one you'd choose for weathering storms. Maybe I wasn't even average here. I couldn't even make a gumbo without following a recipe.

The oil was still gushing when I turned in for the night. I tried not to think about it. Jazz Fest was starting and it would be my first time going. Alone.

Chapter 16

I grew up hearing stories about Jazz Fest from my cousins. They had a "spot" where people knew to look for them. I never joined them because it would've meant leaving L.A. during "pilot season." A pilot was the first episode of a new TV show. By the time the Sundance Film Festival ended every January, L.A. was in high gear through late spring creating dozens and dozens of pilots, most of which would never be aired. But pilot-money was good money and if your show got picked up, cash registers would ring in your ears. It was like a feeding frenzy of work but with only the slimmest of chances that you might get to do the show again or even watch it with your family.

Every year, L.A. would swell with all of the "seasonal" actors who would descend on the city hoping for auditions. Many people in the industry "go where the money is," and the money was definitely in L.A. from February to May. Things had shifted recently as cable-channel-programming had exploded, creating a nearly year-round pilot schedule.

My first week with Marilyn, she got me into three pilot auditions. That was three more than I'd had in my previous seasons. One of them gave me a callback for a comedy called *Down the Hall*. Marilyn was thrilled and used it to get me more auditions.

Then *Down the Hall* called me back again to "test." I hadn't gotten that far before so I wasn't sure what that meant. It was fairly terrifying. There were three versions of me sitting in the waiting room of a network office. I recognized one of them from other auditions and knew she worked. She'd probably done this before. Maybe even this season.

An assistant handed us all contracts on clipboards. We scanned them and signed and initialed them next to adhesive arrows. Working eight days, I'd make enough money to live for a year, more if I was smart and disciplined. Two of our contracts would be torn up after the auditions. It was hard to focus with so many unfamiliar, scary and exciting things happening so quickly.

I went in second. Actors often have no idea how many people will be behind the door, but there are some general numbers. One or two at a first audition. For callbacks, between one and four for a feature and up to six for a commercial. Generally.

I nearly gasped when I opened the door to the small office. There were people dressed in business casual sitting in chairs, on a desk, on the air conditioning vent on the window sill and standing against the walls surrounding my sides. There had to be forty people in that room designed for one executive and a guest. It wasn't even a corner office. It seemed absurd. It was overwhelming. Terrifying.

I knew I wasn't "killin' it," but it was solid work. Marilyn would get okay feedback. Then I sat with the other contender as the woman I knew from other auditions went into the room. Had they laughed that many times during my audition? After an eternity, she came out looking confident. Then they released us and said to stay by our phones. Marilyn said she was proud of me and that the casting directors asked where I'd been hiding and planned to call me in for another project. As rejections go, it was a pretty great one. It actually made me feel optimistic that I'd planted some seeds for future work.

Every year I would burn every end of my candle reading one to five scripts a night and preparing as many auditions. Each audition averaged between three and ten pages. I would break down every scene, rehearse them, choose a wardrobe for each character, hoping to keep things simple since I would have to change in my convertible sports car. Then I'd rehearse some more and go to bed around four. Then I'd paint myself pretty, sit in traffic and rehearse some more.

I'd get callbacks but I never got a pilot. Every year, when my cousins would tell me about Jazz Fest, I'd think, "I did it again. I killed myself for months and never got a pilot." Every year, I'd think, "It's just a week or two. Just go." But every year, I'd have a bunch of auditions and callbacks and I'd keep rolling those dice. That room of forty cramped executives had made me stronger. I held my own when I was way out of my depth and it empowered me. It also gave me optimism that I would keep getting better at auditioning and be less surprised next time. That was true, but I never did get a pilot and I missed Jazz Fest every year.

Until this year.

It was a windy day. I took a bus and instead of the normal mix of residents, tourists and people in black pants and utilitarian black shoes headed to jobs, the bus was filled with people in tie-dye and straw hats toting chairs. I wasn't sure I'd know my stop but I was fairly certain we were all getting off in the same place.

I was always curious about people. The people in front of me were from New Jersey and had been coming for fourteen years. The people behind me were from New York and this was their twenty-eighth year. I suddenly felt like a babe in my own backyard.

The music festival's eleven stages were spread out on the spacious Fairgrounds Race Course. It was like a theatre multiplex but for live music. I wasn't sure where I'd find Lillibette, but I was used to having to figure things out in unknown spaces. I'd been handed the colorful foldout map, but I needed a "you are here" arrow to make sense of it.

Some people crowded around a tall sign board. I was going to have to be one of those people who stare at the giant map and don't know where they are surrounded by an ocean of people living out annual routines. I hated feeling like the tourist in my own home.

Making my way around the crowded track, I was drawn by a band with a Mardi Gras Indian in full plumed-and-beaded splendor. The placard read, "Jockimo's Groove featuring War Chief Juan and Billy Iuso." I meandered into the back of the crowd and stayed to dance for a couple of funky rock songs.

Three Mardi Gras Indian tribes paraded past as the concert was entering its big finish. I couldn't resist all those beads and feathers so I ran to catch them. The wind was insane and the feathered people had a hard time staying upright with gusts whipping their headdresses, giant plumage and heavy beaded panels. I loved the vibrant colors, the creativity and the tedious manual labor that went into the amazing creations. It blew me away every time.

I peeled off and headed for the Acura Stage, the festival's largest and most crowded staging area, in search of Lillibette. She said to look for the windsock shaped like a parrot. I scanned the blanketed field, taking in LSU flags, a blowup doll on a stick and the spinning "Fess head" I'd heard about for decades. The papier-mâché bust of local jazz legend, Professor Longhair, twirled lopsidedly in the wind.

A thin guy with a mop of brown hair spilling out from under a bandana danced wildly in the sandy area in front of the stage. He had three different colored fly swatters tucked into his pants. His probably-drug-induced spasms resembled someone being attacked by bees - but in a kind of fascinating way. At some point, he swung the yellow swatter around like a sword then tucked it between his teeth like a rose.

The Dirty Dozen Brass Band had been around since the 70's. They must've sounded so cutting edge at the time as they pulled jazz in a funkier direction, just as "Fess" had before them. I'd always responded to brass bands, but they were fast becoming some of my favorite local music.

I danced for a few songs then got serious about finding the parrot. Someone tapped my arm and I turned to find Lillibette's sunny smile and bright blue eyes. She shouted something about following her and I nodded like I'd heard her as she made her way toward the concrete path. Turned out we were getting food. I had creole stuffed bread - a ball of bread with seasoned meat inside, and an outstanding shrimp flauta.

We ate over a tall, sticky table meant for standing.

Lillibette wiped a string of melted cheese from my chin. "Can you believe this oil spill?"

"And now they're going to dump some untested chemical in the Gulf."

"Jonathan says it's to sink the oil so they can cover it up."

"Why wouldn't they? They don't live here. They don't eat our food. It's a foreign company who clearly screwed up, and now they're the ones in charge! It's ridiculous."

She chuckled. "Somebody's gettin' rich. That you can bank on."

"I'm thinkin' the Corexit people are busier than usual. But seriously, it's beginnin' to get to me. I keep eating shrimp everyday because I keep assuming there won't be any soon."

"Don't even think that."

"I feel like I'm watching someone bleed to death or somethin'."

Lillibette pulled a wipe from her bag and offered me one. "Maybe the relief well will help."

"It seems like maybe they don't know what they're doing. And the numbers keep changing. Now, they're sayin' there's a third leak and that the leak is five times more than they said it was. They're still lyin', though. They're tryin'a break it to us gently. All that oil spilling out everyday. I would feel bad putting one gallon of oil in the Gulf and they're dumping millions of gallons. Every single day, I stress out thinking they just have to make it stop! And every day, it's worse."

"But today is Jazz Fest so let's just focus on that."

I had no argument for that.

Anders Osborne was onstage when we returned and found Lillibette's blanket. Some fest-friends were holding down the fort. The rest of the cousins weren't attending as frequently now that they'd moved across the lake. They'd been discussing boycotting the fest because of the overcrowding and astronomically-rising ticket prices.

We visited for awhile then left them again to see Sonny Landreth on the Gentilly Stage at the other end of the track. After winding past beer lines and portalets, we found a spot to take in the slide guitarist out of Lafayette. He was soulful, relaxed and clearly an expert. I felt my body go gentle as I swayed to the bluesy music. I smiled at Lillibette. "I love this. Do we have to go back to the other stage? What is it? Pearl Jam? I don't even like them that much."

"My stuff is there."

"Oh, right."

When we got back to the blanket, the crowd was becoming standing room only in anticipation of Pearl Jam. Lillibette folded her chair and rolled her blanket then handed me the pole with the parrot windsock. "Come on."

We pressed through the crowds all the way back to the Gentilly Stage to see Rock and Roll Hall of Famer, Jeff Beck. Like many musicians, I'd met him but had never seen him play live. He was incredible. His bass player was a fierce woman who'd played with Prince's band. Rhonda Smith was like a mighty goddess-warrior whose weapon of choice was the bass. Sexy, strong and stiletto'ed, she all but stole the show with Beck's blessing. It was incredible.

Lillibette offered to drive me home and I offered her a place to stay for the night, but we both declined. Traffic was at a crawl but Lillibette said she needed clean clothes. I could understand that. Jazz Fest could be filthy business.

I caught a streetcar and listened to people comparing their days - which concerts they'd attended and what foods they'd eaten. Apparently I'd missed out on Crawfish Bread, Strawberry Lemonade and something called a Mango Freeze.

As the streetcar rolled past the French Quarter, I remembered meeting Bryan Batt. I remembered the tall, handsome man in the back and suddenly realized I was single again. Another memory popped up before I could stop it, the kid in the hoodie sitting behind Bryan. I jumped up straight in my seat. What if the kid in the hoodie was the same kid from behind the fence? Had he followed us from Bryan's shop and found out where I lived? No, why would he follow me?

What if he had been following Bryan that day on the streetcar? What if he had been the one behind the bushes the night we were shooting the movie? If it was, Trevor was certainly in the clear. Unless they were working together. But why? I'd never heard of tag-team stalkers. That didn't even make sense.

But why would Bryan's stalker follow me? That didn't make sense either. Hoodie-guy had to be the stalker, right? Except tall, handsome guy was on the streetcar too, and he got off when we did as well.

Heck, everyone did - it was the end of the line. Other than the hoodie, there wasn't actually a reason to believe streetcar-guy and fence-guy were the same guy. Sometimes my imagination took flights of fancy.

The camera downloaded photos onto my computer as I took a quick shower. I tried to think of ways to track down someone in a hoodie and came up empty. There had to be a way to stalk a stalker but I didn't have a string to pull on. I was pretty sure Googling "stalker" or "hoodie" wasn't going to yield any results.

I twisted a towel on my head and worked on my Jazz Fest blog post, hoping to blot out unanswered questions.

Chapter 17

Jason was leaving his unit as I came out onto the landing. We took in each other's shoulder bags and both said, "Jazz Fest?" We laughed and agreed to make the trek together.

He looked at my umbrella and rubber sandals. "You're going to need more gear than that."

"It only rained thirty-four days a year in L.A. I bought these sandals here. The umbrella too."

He put his key in the door and looked over his shoulder. "Come in. What you really need is some rain boots." He pointed at his white rubber shrimp boots. "They sell 'em everywhere. You'll start to notice now I've said it. But I do have something for you. Hold on."

I stood in his living room feeling suddenly aware that he was a friend of Tom's. This could look wrong. He could even be one of those nosy neighbors who knows when I'm home - and who I'm spending time with. I tried to think if I had ever seen him hanging out in the Treme house or at Harry's Corner Bar when the whole "gang" was together. Though he and Tom were kickball friends, it was possible they didn't really hang out much.

The room was decorated with the requisite Zulu coconuts and Muses shoes as well as Voodoo candles and local paintings of musicians and wonky homes. I wished my home looked more like this but I was pretty sure it would seem "wannabe" if I forced it. The thing I loved most about these kinds of whimsical, Caribbean-colored, totally local homes was that they were accumulations of culture filled with memories of good times. I was going to have to come by my New Orleanian home the same way everyone else did, by living here.

Jason came out carrying a heavy-duty hooded rain poncho. It was far nicer than the one he had on. "My ex left it here when she bailed. She liked nice things so it's a good one."

The poncho was fantastic from a utilitarian point of view, but if he'd said that in L.A., "nice things" would mean something from Prada or Burberry's. I kept finding my values reaffirmed in this city.

It was raining pretty hard and I was instantly glad Jason had offered the poncho. The air had been heavy with the smell of chemicals for days as they performed controlled burns on the oil spill. It kept reminding me of the Malibu fire of '93 that blotted out the sun for days and created a "snow" of ash. We had to use windshield wipers to clear the remains of people's furniture, clothes, photos and heirlooms. It was gruesome.

Though rivulets were already making their way inside the neckline of my hoodie, I was grateful the rain was cleansing our air of the odor of failure and destruction. There was a chance we could have a whole day of not thinking about the oil soaking our wetlands and killing our wildlife and the Corexit poisoning our food chain.

I was nervous that Jason might be leading me

right to Tom's unwitting group. Neither of us had mentioned the break up. But I couldn't think of an argument for grabbing a bite together before we hit the stages. We stood at a slick, wet table and split a combo platter. We divided the tied satchel of dough baked full of crawfish and saucy yumminess and an oyster fabulous thing in an individual phyllo pastry pie. Luckily, there were three of my favorite dish, the crawfish beignets.

Jason used his rain soaked hand to wipe his mouth. I used a napkin that turned to pulp on my face. He laughed. "I'm heading to Gentilly. You're welcome to join."

I wiped my mouth with my wet hand a few more times.

"You got it all. Don't worry."

I thought about lying and saying that Lillibette was here somewhere, if only so he wouldn't worry about me, but I decided to tell the truth. "There's a bunch of things here I've never seen. Not just the music, all the artisans and stuff. The carousel. Today's the last day so I'm going to do some exploring."

We hugged, then he yelled over his shoulder, "Happy Jazz Fest!"

"Happy Jazz Fest!"

Tents created an outdoor mall of local painters, sculptors, photographers and clothing designers. I went to Paris alone once for work. I thought I would hate seeing the Louvre, Musee de Rodin, the Eiffel Tower and other manmade wonders by myself, but it was actually fairly magical. I was the type of person who could stare at something for a long time trying to figure it all out so I luxuriated in not having to share my attention with someone impatient or disinterested.

There was an area behind the tents dedicated to local tribes of Native Americans. A group visiting from somewhere else (I think I heard Michigan) beat rhythmically in a drum circle while chanting. Their wives sat on foldout chairs beside the stage holding children on their laps. The rain had nearly stopped and it was becoming easy to relax and enjoy the day.

Competing drum beats came from the track where a social aid and pleasure club was leading a second line parade. I caught up as the fierce women in white pantsuits and hats strutted past pumping white umbrellas decorated with blue sequins and feather boas. The woman dancing in the front wore royal blue with a matching fedora. A whistle hung from her lip like a cigarette. She looked like a boss, like a queen in glittery high-heeled blue boots.

Further down the path, the pink-corseted Pussyfooters danced in white combat boots. I ran to watch them pass then spotted Christine Miller, the tour guide, in the group. I waved to her and she waved back. The tall, warrior woman next to her in the pink and orange mohawk-headdress waved too so I waved back. Their short, ruffled skirts flounced into the distance and I was finally ready to see some music.

Trombone Shorty was commanding the Gentilly Stage. He was one of the locals who played himself on HBO's *Treme*. When Trombone Shorty was at Jazz Fest at three or four years old, the legendary Bo Diddley invited him onstage. Though I hadn't seen it yet, there was apparently a photo of him playing the trombone, three times his own size, with Bo Diddley listening in the background. Trombone Shorty was plenty tall now, and handsome to boot.

I tapped a shoulder in front of me. "How long's he been playin'?"

"He introduced the band again so I think this is his last song."

The band was amazing and I loved the song. We all raised our hands and yelled "hey!" on cue during the instrumental's chorus. I wanted it to go on forever and joined everyone in screaming for more.

The guy in front of me jolted, "That's Mystikal! Look, comin' onstage. That's him. Dang man, he just got out." He shouted to his friends, "Y'all, that's Mystikal fresh off a six year stint."

I wasn't entirely sure what the fuss was about until he broke into his hit, *Shake Ya Azz* and the crowd went wild dancing in the mud.

On the way to the Acura Stage was the carousel I'd heard about from my cousins. Small and wooden, a live band sat in the center providing the music as men manually pushed the carousel around and around. They got it moving surprisingly fast. It was all very simple and "green." Watching the carousel spin, I thought of how much we complicate the very things we're trying to make more simple. I'd made a piece of toast in my broiler the other day instead of my toaster and it was golden brown with caramelized puddles of butter. So much better. Progress didn't always equal improvement. Newer wasn't always better here.

Throughout my life, there had been movies and songs that had "saved me." Van Morrison made one of those songs, the one that helped me keep my heart open when it would have made more sense to grow bitter. As the rain began to pour in earnest, Morrison played the crowd favorites, *Brown Eyed Girl* and *Moondance.* In L.A., people generally stayed in and avoided driving when it rained. It was hard to imagine a crowd of them getting soaked to the undies and dancing in mud. A beach ball came my way and I instinctively hit it. A spray of water bounced off the slick surface and into my face as it launched into the air and back into the crowd.

Van Morrison sang beautiful songs beautifully and played a wide variety of instruments but he never played *I'll Be You're Lover, Too.* Swaying in the rain surrounded by fellow music lovers, it occurred to me that maybe I didn't need a song to keep my heart open anymore. I felt alive and connected and happy almost all of the time lately. I wasn't even feeling all the abandonment and fear that should've accompanied Tom dumping me.

With no one to coordinate with, I wandered until horns drew me to another stage. TBC Brass Band was playing Michael Jackson's *Billy Jean.* Splashing mud and water, the fit jumping guy with the black-and-gold sash that read, "Dancing Man 504" was putting on a show in the crowd. I'd seen him dancing in the street before a Saints game one night. He smiled at me and I joined his group of revelers for a song, rain sticking the rubber poncho to my thighs.

It was getting late and I still hadn't decided where was I going to end my Jazz Fest. The Tulane alumni crowd usually hit The Radiators. Everyone else went to the Neville Brothers. Not being a "true local," the opportunity to see living legend B.B. King seemed

166

irresistible. There was no way to have all the experiences being offered. That happened a lot in New Orleans.

A hand on my shoulder startled me.

"Sorry, I didn't mean to scare you." Trevor smiled warmly.

"Oh, hey!"

"Hey. Happy Jazz Fest."

"Happy Jazz Fest." I gathered myself. "I'm kinda glad I'm running into you. I have a weird question."

"I'm intrigued. Fire away."

"You remember when we were getting ready to do your stunt and there was somebody behind the bushes? Did you get a look at him? Did you happen to see what he was wearing or anything?"

"That's all I saw. He was in a hoodie so I couldn't see his face or hair. For all I know, it was a tall woman."

"Do you remember the color? What it was made of?"

"Sweatshirt material. Why? You're kinda freaking me out."

"No, it's just---"

"Another weird thing happened a couple days ago." He lowered his voice and got closer to my ear. "We're on another movie now and someone stole something out of Bryan's trailer."

"Are you sure? Things get moved all the time on a set."

"It was in his trailer. There's no reason for anyone but wardrobe to be in there. I gave him a leather journal to thank him for getting me hired again and it went missing from a drawer in the bedroom side table. He said he'd written some thoughts in it and remembered marking the page with the spine ribbon and putting it into the drawer when he was called to set. That's the last anyone saw of it."

"That's kinda creepy."

He nodded his head. "Very."

"Was there anything else in the journal? Anything about it that would give it value?"

"No, I mean it was nice, it was leather-bound. But it wasn't particularly special. And the only thing in it was my inscription."

"Weird." Why would anyone steal a nearly empty journal? "Seems personal."

"Bryan's in good spirits but I can tell it's beginning to get to him. Couldn't blame him if he got a little paranoid."

"Well, not to freak you out further, but I saw a guy in a hoodie near my house the other day."

"Now you sound paranoid."

"In the bushes." Figured that would seem familiar. "In my neighbor's yard actually, looking over the fence as I was coming home. It was grey, the hoodie. He was my height and fairly slender. He ran when I saw him."

"At your house?"

"My neighbor's actually. But yeah."

Trevor looked troubled. "Did you get mugged recently? Lose your I.D. or anything with an address?"

"No, nothing like that. But, it could have been anything. A guest looking for a key or someone trying to break into their house or whatever."

"You got a funny way of comforting yourself."

"Whatever it takes, right? Honestly, Bryan should ask around and make sure no one moved the journal. Just seems very dramatic to sneak onto a set and into a star's trailer just to take an almost-empty book."

He nodded. "Maybe so. Probably, right? Either way, let me give you my number in case anything else comes up."

We exchanged information and a wet hug, then he headed off it the direction of The Radiators.

Why would anyone take an empty journal? It seemed an escalation over slipping envelopes or standing behind bushes. It was actual trespassing. Whoever it was couldn't have known whether Bryan had written in it and it seemed unlikely Bryan would've signed a journal entry so it was hard to imagine any financial motivation, even among those who collected *Mad Men* memorabilia.

The Acura staging area was less crowded than I'd left it. The weather and two weeks of celebrating music had taken their toll. Still, it was inspiring that people walked for miles, carrying packs of plastic weather gear, even changes of clothes, to be here. People here were willing to sweat, get stung by bugs, wade through mud and puddles, get covered in wind blown sand and spend entire days drenched in rain or cooked by sun just to enjoy some music. These city folk were not like any I'd encountered before. I was used to worrying about fashion and hair. I was used to having a clean, dry seat and a roof over my head for concerts. Thinking about the oil spill and all that our region might have to face, I took comfort in knowing that among the many things that made this place unique was the people's willingness to be uncomfortable.

The Nevilles played local favorites like *Pocky Way* and *Fiyo on the Bayou* as well as some of those slow, pretty Aaron Neville ballads. I was sure it was sacrilege but I slipped out early and headed over to B.B. King's concert tent.

At eighty-four, King sat through his set but he remained vibrant and soulful. I stayed for a couple songs but the rain was really coming down, and the tent was too crowded to enter so it was time to call it.

When it was all sung and done, I made my way home to watch HBO's *Treme* and work on my blog post. Though I couldn't help thinking about why anyone would want an empty journal, stalking stalkers would have to wait for another day.

Chapter 18

With both football and Carnival season behind us and festival season winding down, the dog days of summer began to take hold. Local musicians would be leaving town to tour. Bugs and heat would drive many indoors. I tried watching comedies on TV to take my mind off not working now that I had nothing but time on my hands, but it was getting harder to ignore the BP disaster. A constant crawl on the bottom of the screen listed numbers. There was a number for if you found an affected animal, a number for those who found fouled land and a number for those willing to volunteer a boat and services to "Vessels of Opportunity."

It had only been a few weeks since the Deepwater explosion, but our illusions of this disaster playing out differently with a "hope and change" President were dashed and that familiar feeling of being lied to and abandoned settled over the region again. The oil had reached our shores, saturated our marshes and coated wildlife. And no one had any idea how to stop it. There was a website accepting suggestions.

The air smelled of burning Crayons. Some mixture of burning oil and chemicals. I'd stopped eating seafood. Many restaurants weren't serving shrimp anymore. Oysters were getting scarce as well.

People comforted themselves with talk of oil being "natural" and biodegradable but we all knew the Corexit had changed everything. They'd never tested it for use underwater. We would be the lab rats.

I could almost feel the oil gushing from the well. It made me anxious. I'd fuss at my TV, cursing Coast Guard representatives, politicians and polite-sounding Brits from BP. I could try to ignore the images of a murderous rig explosion and consumptive oil slicks. They were almost too big and movie-like to be real. That could be comforting in a way. The "24 hour news cycle" meant the images were available any time the TV was on. The repetition could make it seem like a "new normal." That, too, could be comforting in a way. Extreme anxiety always pressed people into extreme coping techniques. The body would involuntarily find ways to return to feeling comfortable, and the brain could justify many otherwise-insane thoughts to feel in control of the situation.

Though I understood how it all worked, I still had to battle the same involuntary reactions everyone else did. I used understanding and dissecting problems as a coping technique. If I was thinking and puzzling, I wouldn't be tuned into what I was feeling. But feelings have their way of breaking through. For some, their dreams speak, for others it's their health or temper. For me, it was "vision burps." I'd be taking a bath or drinking a glass of water and suddenly see a drop of red. I couldn't say that it was blood, but it was always red. Then another drop. And another. As the drops sped up, they quit disappearing into the clear water and began changing the color of the water. All of the water was affected. That was the image I couldn't erase, the feeling that wouldn't be silenced. It was fear and despair. And anger.

That unmitigated joy we felt when the Saints won the Super Bowl in the middle of Mardi Gras had found its lid. We would go back to being "The City that Care Forgot" and finding our joys where we could. I was glad I'd already navigated so many high highs and low lows in L.A. I was already practiced at having a good day in the face of failure and rejection. I hoped it wouldn't be much harder to remain upbeat in the face of ruin and abandonment.

I tried not to think about breathing burning oil and Corexit. I tried not to think about our food chain and being lab rats. I didn't want to be afraid of my food, water and air. It seemed too apocalyptic.

I was trying to care about a rerun of *Just Shoot Me!* when my phone rang. Tom. A jolt ran through me. "Hey!"

"Hey Slim. Where y'at?"

"I'm good. Freaked out by all the oil stuff. You must really be at wit's end by now."

"Yeah, it's been rough lately."

We were quiet a moment, long enough for me to realize I wasn't sure I wanted him back if he'd had a change of heart. I had a rule about people who were stupid enough to dump me being too stupid for me. "Are you okay?"

He was quiet long enough for me to want to speak just to break the silence, but I waited. His voice was small. "My dad died."

I wanted to say, "Oh my gosh! Are you okay? Do you need anything?" I stopped myself and took a breath. "I'm so sorry, Tom. I'm so sorry." I stopped myself from saying, "It'll be okay eventually. He's gone Home. He had a good, long life. Be grateful he's not suffering anymore." I breathed and said, "That's terrible. I can't even imagine how overwhelmed you must feel with all of this happening."

"Thanks." He chuckled. "Yeah, I haven't been much of a good-time guy. But I've been keepin' up with my drinkin'. I've got that goin' for me."

I chuckled. "Can't say as I blame you."

"The funeral is tomorrow and Boudoux and Margie and Nancy and everyone's comin'."

"That's good. It'll be good for you to have some support."

He took a breath. "I debated calling... but honestly, I'd like you there."

It was my turn to be quiet too long.

"If it's too weird, don't worry about it. I just wanted you to know."

"No. I mean, yes, of course I'll go. That's fine. It'll be good to see everyone."

Tom's voice shifted. "I'll text you the address. It's at noon."

"Okay. I'll see you tomorrow."

"See ya, Slim."

The phone beeped. Sofia. "Perfect timing. I just clicked over from Tom inviting me to his dad's funeral. And I'm going. Tomorrow."

"Wait. Like a date?"

"No." I quickly replayed the conversation in my head. "I don't think so. No."

"So, he didn't just ask you to be his date at the funeral? Wait, didn't he go to funerals a minute ago?"

"Memorials. I don't think they ever found any of those guys. But, yeah. Four, I think."

She closed a door, probably to go outside for privacy. "That's a lot. And he's the environmental guy, right?"

"Wetlands, yeah."

"Sucks to be him."

His text came in and I resisted wanting to write him something comforting.

Sofia laughed. I couldn't imagine why. "Remember that time?" She could barely talk for all the laughing. "We were at a party in Malibu and those guys came up just as we were talking about somebody dying, I forget who."

"It's a long list of possibilities."

She was laughing so hard that it was mostly silent with brief gasps for air. "And they just..." More laughing, "Walked away."

We both laughed and I pitched in, "Then we tried that with all the other guys that hit on us that night. We'd just talk about death."

She'd escalated to full cry-laughing. "And they'd scatter like roaches in the light." Her voice was pinched - almost indecipherable. "Hey ladies!"

I used a somber voice. "Death."

"Run!"

I'd loved Sofia so much for so long that it was like habit but I never took moments like these for granted. These were the moments reserved for old friends. I'd just moved and put myself in a position to be surrounded entirely by new friends.

Sofia calmed herself. "That was hilarious. It was so consistent. Death. Bye!" She laughed a little more.

"It's weird he called, right? Are you okay?"

"I think I'm fine, but it's a little weird."

"Okay, so this is why I called. I thought about what he said about being a dime-a-dozen guy. It's good news. Think about it. What if he's right? What if being a nice boyfriend is normal there?"

"I would argue but I have no evidence against your theory so far."

"So, if they're a dime-a-dozen, you can be picky, right? You don't really want the drinking good-time-guy, do you? I mean, shouldn't that be a bare minimum that your guy not drink himself drunk all the time?"

I thought about that. Everyone had flaws but she was right, I tried that one and it didn't go well. "I think I have no argument for that."

"He's right, you didn't move from all this to get wrapped up in a good-time-guy who goes to more funerals than concerts. It's bad timing. I think he's telling you the truth."

"Death. Run!"

We laughed.

She settled again. "Maybe he was just 'Green Gloves Guy.' Seriously though. I mean, go to the funeral if you want but I'd take his word for it."

"You know, I did get to date a lot of extraordinary men in L.A. Amazing unique-in-the-world men... totally incapable of having relationships."

"Right. So, if being fun and nice is a dime-a-dozen there, maybe the guys there are more ordinary in the world but amazing at being in relationships."

"From your lips to God's ears."

"Stranger things have happened than a nice guy

meeting a nice girl and them being nice to each other."

I laughed. "It still sounds kinda crazy when you say it out loud. But, you're right. It's not a ridiculous goal."

"Think about other stuff. It'll happen when it happens and when it does, you're not even going to care anymore that you had to go through all of this to meet him."

"I'm not going to mind marrying a man who yelled at me for years then dating decades of disasters when I wasn't just alone, alone, alone? That would have to be one heck of a guy."

"Water finds its own level."

I thought about that and decided to hope she was right. "I know what else we can talk about. That actor I worked with who has the awesome shop, the one who gave me the wax seal? He's being stalked. His stunt guy said someone stole a journal out of his trailer. For like, no reason. All it had in it was one entry Bryan had just written that no one knew about. Well, and Trevor's inscription. It was a gift. He'd just given it to him. But like, on Ebay or whatever, that would make it less valuable to have Trevor's signature and not Bryan's. I just can't think of one reason to steal it. And only Trevor and Bryan even knew it existed."

"That's weird."

"Right?"

"You'll figure it out."

"How? It took forever to even figure out the symbol on the chandelier was a well. And I still have no idea why it keeps showing up all over my life."

"Yeah, but that's like a hundred year old mystery. That's like a super-cold case. It's practically archeology."

We laughed. Her voice got comforting. "You can figure all this stuff out. The symbol, the stalker, all of it. It's pretty much all you do. You figure out stuff about people for a living. Didn't you say acting was about details? Just think it out. Why would you steal that journal? You'll figure it out. This is what you're good at--- Oh, shoot. My battery's dying. Where's my---"

She was gone.

Why would I steal that journal? I opened my computer and a browser window. I had no idea where to start. At least I knew it wasn't Trevor. I was glad I hadn't jumped to conclusions and told Bryan my suspicions about him. L.A. had taught me the value of credibility. It probably wasn't the handsome guy in the back of the streetcar who was too tall to be the guy in the bushes. The guy in the grey hoodie seemed a good conclusion to jump to, but why would he risk arrest for an empty journal? Why would anyone? It had to have a value I couldn't see. I was missing something.

What if it was a fan? Some fans confused actors with the characters they played. I supposed it could be flattering to think you'd done such a good job acting that you'd actually tricked the person into thinking you were the character. It apparently happened a lot with TV actors that played the same character for years, especially soap actors. I'd heard it was all fun and games "until the fan starts yelling about something your character did to some other character they like better."

Back in acting class in L.A., I'd done a scene with a longtime soap star. She told me that one woman had grabbed and attacked her. She was screaming about the character cheating on her husband while he was in a wheelchair.

Other fans got so confused about reality that they thought the person they admired was in some sort of personal relationship with them. It could be as innocuous as thinking a celebrity would remember having met them in an elevator seven years ago. Or it could get as odd as a fan thinking the person was speaking directly to them during interviews. Those were the ones to worry about.

Bryan was best known for his closeted-gay character on *Mad Men*. Though Bryan was out, it was possible someone might identify with the character and get confused. Or maybe it was someone with a hero complex. Maybe a confused fan who was out-and-proud wanted to help Bryan come out. Or maybe the fan thought they were in love.

I'd never seen *Mad Men* and I was a fan of Bryan's work so maybe it was a different character that inspired someone's confusion. I clicked the IMDbPro tab and entered Bryan's name. As I scrolled the titles, I had no idea what to look for - not even a guess.

I needed another angle. If all the guys in hoodies were the same guy, there seemed to be some connection to me - or possibly my neighbor. I clicked on the movie Bryan and I had done together. Over fifty actors and almost a hundred people in the crew. Most, of course, were men. Very few had photos. I had no idea what to do next. I clicked the movie Bryan had done before ours, another local production. Less than thirty actors and a crew of fifty-two.

I skipped the executives and top crew and clicked the first assistant I came across. I scanned their credits looking for our movie. This was going to take forever.

My normally dormant phone rang again. Taffy. "Hey! How are you?"

"Good. I'm good. You good?"

"Oil thing sucks but yeah, I'm good. What's goin' on?"

"Chiffon and me been talkin'. Think it's time to sell Mama's house."

"The Treme house? I love that house."

"Us too, but we never gonna live there. We got lives other places, ya heard me? Just talkin' about it, but we thought you should know with you havin' the chandelier."

"Oh."

"Might have to stay with you awhile if that's alright."

"Yeah, of course." I liked feeling like part of their legacy. "I'm kinda used to havin' it around now, tell you the truth. I like the rainbows it puts on the walls."

"Good. Thank you for that. We appreciate it."

"Hey Taffy, outa curiosity, was your great-grandmother's name Matilda or maybe Persephone?"

She laughed. "I don't think so. They called her Mama T. I figured her name started with a 't' or it was short for somethin'."

"Like what? Y'all have any family names like

that, either start with a 't' or somethin' it could be short for?"

"We had some second cousin or somethin' what went by TiTi but it was that her brother couldn't say Theresa when he was little."

"Could it be short for Matilda? Does that make sense?"

I could hear her dog in the background. "That'd most likely be Tildy. Even if you shorten Tildy, you get D. Why do you want her name to be Matilda so bad?"

I laughed. "I don't. I mean, I do, I did, but I was just asking. I played a character named Cassandra."

"Yeah, Chiffon told me Lillibette said you got another movie. That's great."

I kept being reminded that for most people it was special to get work on a movie. "Thanks."

"With your niece and your mama too? That's what I heard. Next time, tell 'em you got a cousin wants to be in a movie. We could pass for cousins if you use some imagination."

I chuckled. "Yeah, but seriously? You're a twin. Twins are good. If I ever hear anyone needs twins, I'll mention y'all if you're serious."

Her dog barked again. "Jojo, hush! Naw, I ain't serious. I wouldn't even begin to know what to do with myself. Lillibette said it's hours of sittin' around."

"Yeah. There's an old saying that they pay us to wait, the acting we do for free. But wait, so I was researching for this Cassandra character and I looked up the name and it said she was a prophetess in Greek mythology who was the daughter of Hecuba, like

Mama Heck. And Cassandra's brother was named Paris like UncaParis."

"What?"

"So then I looked up Hecuba and she was the daughter of Eunoe."

She was quiet a minute. "And Eunoe was the daughter of Matilda?"

"No, she was a nymph, the daughter of a river god and maybe Persephone who was the daughter of Zeus and a harvest goddess. Matilda I got from a different story. In that one, Eunoe is the name of a place in the afterlife where memories of your good deeds are strengthened on your way to the Garden of Eden."

"Jojo! Hush up!" I heard her clap her hand against her thigh. "It's just the neighbor cat. Go lay down. Lay down." She was quiet a moment and I imagined a stare-down. "Okay, you were sayin' about Matilda."

"Right, so Matilda was the name of the person who helped the souls on their journey to the Garden of Eden, including through Eunoe, the river of good deeds. Look, I knew it was a stretch."

"Mama T's all I got but that's cool you found all that. You know better'n most that Mama thought names oughta mean somethin'. I wonder if she knew all that."

"I seriously doubt it. She woulda told you. She'da known 'em if they were in the Bible, but these names are from things like Dante and Homer. I'm still tryin'a figure out how Mama Eunoe's mother knew any of this. Wasn't she a slave? Why would she know of a river in Dante's Divine Comedy or a relatively obscure nymph in Greek mythology?"

"Jojo, don't even think about it. I swear, this dog is like having a third child. And the worst part is it's growin' on me. Sits on my feet on cold nights. Looks at me like he's listenin'. Kids are tryin'a get 'im to beg but so far, I'm the one doin' all the beggin'."

"I saw 'im on Facebook. I see how they got ya to say yes. Those eyes."

"Named 'im Jojo for those Richard Pryor eyes. Look like the ones on the DVD box for *Jo Jo Dancer*."

"Now I'm going to have to look that up. But wait, names. So, you don't know anything about Mama T's name? Or Mama Eunoe? Honestly, wasn't Mama Eunoe born a slave? If Mama Heck's real name is Hecuba, how did Eunoe know to name her that? And how did Mama Heck know to name her children Cassandra and Paris. That part I know for sure is real. That happened. Cassandra and Paris are siblings in the mythology. It's weird, right? It seems like it should mean something. Sassy was so adamant about your names meaning somethin' that she put it in her will. That's what she willed to you. She said, 'I did all I could to give y'all a name that meant somethin'. I understand if that isn't enough. Follow your hearts and you will never betray me. Except with the chandelier. Take your best care of the chandelier.'"

"Dang, you remembered that by heart?"

I chuckled. "It happens sometimes. Job side effect. But think about it. We assumed she talking about you finding your birth mother but what if she was talking about your heritage?"

"She got us in a laundromat, we don't really have a heritage."

I realized I was treading into sensitive terrain and that I might end up speaking from ignorance. "No, I understand what you're sayin' but there's more stuff passed from one generation to another than just genes. I've got my dad's nose and my mom's legs, but I also have my dad's work ethic and my mom's open-mindedness. My dad comes from a long line of overachievers, and he lived that culture in front of me and modeled it for me and it affected me and helped shape me. My mom was college educated because her mom was college educated. Her mom was a farmer's daughter born at the turn of the century, but her farmer dad sent her to college. That's open-minded. That's having all the same information everyone else has and coming to a different conclusion. And thinking that women deserved a college education became normal in my family by the time I was born. I assumed I'd go to college and just thought about which one or what major or whatever. That's a heritage too. It's a culture. Sassy gave you a culture. I've had your red beans so I know I'm right on this."

"No, I hear ya. I do. I feel that. Don't get me wrong, I'm glad you found out who our birth mother was, but this has been a confusin' year with Mama passin' and everything. Didn't know I was gonna have to think so much deep stuff and feel so many feelings."

"I'm sorry. I'm just thinkin' thoughts. I didn't mean to keep pressin' on your pain."

She took a breath. "I'm good. So, you're sayin' what if she meant she gave us a name that would lead to our heritage?"

I smiled. It didn't sound as crazy as I feared it would. "Basically."

"So Cassandra's children were Chiffon and Taffeta?"

"No." Maybe it was crazy after all.

"Violet and Azure?"

"No, Teledamus and Pelops."

She laughed. "Talledega and Peanuts?"

I laughed too. "You can see why she failed to burden you with that name, Talledega."

"Tally for short."

"Of course, Tal."

"Call me T."

We laughed. I heard the chandelier jangle down the hall. "Mama Heck's at it again."

"I don't know how you sleep under that thing knowin' it has a mind of it's own. Never did that at Mama's house. Special for you."

"I'm used to it. New normal. So you can't think of any reason they'd pass Greek mythology as their heritage?"

"Chiffon might know. She and Mama talked about books sometimes. And she was always Mama Heck's favorite so maybe she knows some stories." Jojo's dog tags jangled in the distance. "I gotta go. Jojo's givin' me them big eyes. I'm'a take 'im for a 'w' 'a' 'l' 'k.' Oh, his head just titled like he's listenin'. I know you can't spell, Jojo. No use tryin' trick me with them Pryor eyes. I gotta go, Charlotte. Wish me luck with this dog. Can't believe I let them strap me with this. Come on, Jojo. We goin' out. Charlotte, you gotta see 'im. He's bouncin' like a wind-up toy. I gotta go."

I hoped Chiffon would know something. I'd put a name and face to their birth mother but she'd only passed them genes, not the story of how they came to be raised. I kept feeling they both mattered. Sassy hadn't passed them their springy, supple "good hair" curls or brown eyes with golden flecks, but she had passed all she knew and all she was. That had to be just as important. More maybe. I couldn't know what it felt like to know so little about my birth mother and have no clue to a father. I was thinking the privileged thoughts of someone who knew I had my dad's nose and my mom's legs. But, knowing that meant knowing that it didn't make me who I was.

I walked toward the bedroom reciting Sassy's will. "I did all I could to give y'all a name that meant somethin'. I understand if that isn't enough. Follow your hearts and you will never betray me. Except with the chandelier. Take your best care of the chandelier." Why did it have to hang?

The moon glinted off the chandelier. The crystals stood straight out like a porcupine. I stopped myself from flipping the light switch.

"Mama Heck?"

I don't know what I expected to happen.

"Mama Heck. Is that you?"

Nothing.

"Mama Heck. It's Helen's baby, Charlotte. Miss Henrietta's grandbaby." I laughed. "Did you call her Miss Henry for short?"

The crystals began trembling. Small trembles at first, then busy enough to rattle. I started to feel scared. The crystals shook, convulsed, then dropped, swinging and tinkling against each other. It was the same noise I'd heard earlier. I turned on the light. One crystal was still sticking out. Was it the scratched one? The one Taffy said made Mama Heck realize she truly owned the chandelier if she was allowed to scratch it?

My heart was pounding. I walked across the hardwood floor and reached my fingers toward the crystal expecting it to drop like it had when Taffy tried to touch it.

The crystal was vibrating slightly. I took a breath and gingerly clasped it between by fingers. The vibration stopped. I turned it in the light and found the checkmark-shaped scratch then dropped it like a hot coal.

The crystal swung back and forth as my breath got shallow. I left quickly, turning out the light on my way. Maybe I would sleep on the couch.

Chapter 19

Tom was talking to Boudeux when I walked into the funeral home. He spotted me and smiled. "You came."

"I did."

We hugged and I wished I could make this day go away for him. Boudoux grabbed a hug as well. "You look beautiful." He smacked Tom's arm. "That's what you're supposed to say when a goddess like this enters a room."

I chuckled. "Maybe you go easy on him today?"

Tom smiled and took my hand. "I'm glad you're here. Thanks for that. I'll see you after."

It was standing-room only in the hall. I joined Nancy and Margie in the back, and we exchanged hugs and whispered greetings.

It was a very traditional service, somber and full of praise for the life lived. By the end, I was sad I'd never known him. It seemed I'd missed out on a fun, interesting man. I reminded myself that it was his liver that got him.

It was odd to finally meet Tom's mother afterward. She was gracious, warm even, despite the day's events and the hell I knew she'd gone through recently. She introduced me to neighbors and friends of hers from church. She was so gracious that I began wondering if Tom had gotten around to telling her we weren't dating anymore. Maybe she was just another perfect southern hostess. Through the glass door, I could see Boudoux and the gang sitting at a white wrought iron table full of cocktails. I waved and excused myself from the confusion of finally feeling part of the family.

"You're empty-handed. What can I get you?" Boudoux was always a host.

"I'm good. I can't stay long." I could've.

"At least let me get you a water."

I smiled. "Yes, thank you. I'd love a water."

He seemed happy to have something to do.

Margie motioned to the seat next to her. "Stay a minute. I'm leaving soon, too."

They all joked easily, swapped Jazz Fest stories and argued over whether gumbo served over potato salad was "the best way" or "just wrong." The Lafayette potato-salad crowd was outnumbered.

It would be hard to lose all these friends at once. They were Tom's and that was that, but they were also most of the friends I'd made since moving. I now saw the flaw in that plan. Maybe it was time to let it all go and hope the physics of nature abhorring a vacuum would bring me more friends soon.

It was a lovely home full of lovely people but I began feeling more and more aware that I had no real place there. "It was so great seein' y'all but I've gotta go."

There were protests and hugs. Tom walked me through the house and to the front porch. I wasn't sure what to wish for.

"Thanks for comin', Slim. It meant a lot."

I wasn't sure why. I was used to endgames and

alternative motives and stayed alert to clues of what he wanted from me. "It was my pleasure. I mean, not the funeral. I mean... You know what I mean."

We hugged the hug of longtime friends, people who care about each other. We pulled away and looked at each other.

"Thanks, Slim. Be good."

"Yeah. You too. Thanks for inviting me."

He turned and reached for the doorknob just as Margie popped out. "Oh hey! I was looking for you." She grabbed Tom up into a hug. "Don't go in hiding. We're here, okay?"

He went inside and I let my heart sink.

Margie's car was in front of mine in the long line on the street. She dug through her purse. "You heading home?"

"Yeah."

"You doing okay?"

"I guess. Life is funny sometimes."

"You're gonna be fine. You know that, right?"

I slipped my key into the lock. "Yeah. Sure."

"He's a good guy but he's not your guy. You must know that."

"Seems to be the story. I guess I just hoped he was wrong so I wouldn't have to be single again."

She laughed. "I hear that. Seriously though, Charlotte, you're going to be fine. I get it, I lived in L.A. Trust me, it's better here. Even if you have to date, it'll be fun. You"ll see."

"Thanks. Seriously. I needed to hear that from someone who might actually know."

She pulled her keys out, hugged me and got into her car. A motor hummed as the window lowered.

"Come see me play sometime. Bring a date." She waved as the car pulled away.

I used to cry in my car sometimes in L.A. I felt so unsafe letting people see my weaknesses there and crying alone at home seemed like a rabbit hole. Car trips had endings. The radio was playing *I'm Yours,* and I was driving away from a man I could've loved, but no tears came. Instead, a calm took over - the kind that comes with closure. Tom's childhood home disappeared in the rearview. As the Superdome peeked over the interstate, tears finally fell. Happy-cry tears. I was in love. I was in love with my city.

The chandelier was behaving itself and I finally had a moment to stalk the stalker. Instead of opening my laptop, I let my head rest against the arm of the couch and closed my eyes. I wasn't sure it mattered why the stalker was stalking. The motive would fill in the story and might be a key to the stalker's identity, but it was unwise to even begin guessing a motive before knowing what we were dealing with.

What was a stalker? A people hunter. A tracker. In some ways, they were like detectives or private eyes. I'd played those before. What did hunters do? They would lie in wait, hidden, observing, hoping for an opportunity to strike. Or they would track their prey and ambush them. But this hidden huntsman wanted its prey to know he existed. He'd sent the photo so Bryan would know he was watching him. Since there seemed to be no inherent value in the stolen journal, it was possible he only took it to let Bryan know he'd been in his trailer.

Every hunter had to start somewhere. Where might the stalker have started his tracking? Stalkers might collect a damning amount of information before you even knew they existed, but even hunters left a trail. I just had to figure out where to look.

I sat up and opened my computer and went to Bryan's IMDb page again. I clicked the movie he'd done just before ours and scanned the names. I wasn't sure what I was looking for. Keith Dalton was listed in "Miscellaneous Crew" as a Production Assistant. That must've been the set where he'd taken the photo of Bryan and Trevor in matching suits with yellow pocket squares.

I clicked the next movie and scanned the names looking for repetitions. Brett Bateman was a Picture Car Coordinator who'd worked on both as had Set Dresser Jillian Moore and Still Photographer Peter Dupre. Trevor was Bryan's double, as usual. And Keith Dalton was listed as a P.A. again. I checked the movie listed just before that one and scanned the names again. This time, I knew what I was looking for. There was Trevor again and, boom, there was good old Keith Dalton again. Perfect. I finally had a suspect, and he was dead.

I clicked his name anyway. There were the two movies he'd done with Bryan and the one he'd done with me, *Stealing Tomorrow.* I clicked that movie and scanned again. Apparently, Brett Bateman was the Picture Car Coordinator again. And Trevor had done stunts. It was pretty normal for me not to meet most of the crew since I usually only worked a few days. Most of my "work days" were spent trying to get more work.

I searched for the "missing kid" file and opened the photos inside. A selfie of Keith at base camp with me in the background wearing a navy robe and reading my script. A long, crowded lunch table with Bryan and Trevor in matching suits. Teenaged Keith on a dirt bike. It seemed odd that those were the only three personal photos. No friends. No out-drinking shots. No cute girl smiling for him. Just two work photos and a dirt bike.

The dirt bike seemed a little "macho" for Keith. His frame was slight and his face was boyish. I hadn't downloaded the photo of him they'd used on the news so I jumped onto Facebook to remember it. His face was daintier than I remembered. It hit me that he might not be straight. But, I used to think that a lot in L.A. Coming from the East Coast, I was just used to a more alpha-male world so "metrosexuals" threw me.

Keith's timeline had a few new posts. A link to the obituary, a reposting of the news story with the video and an article about the release date for the first movie he did with Bryan. The obituary listed family and his high school then described him as having gone to New Orleans 'to pursue his dream of being a stuntman.'"

A stuntman? P.A. wasn't exactly an entry level position for a stuntman. That said, stunt crews were very hard to break into. Someone needed to vouch for you. Maybe he'd hoped Bryan would, or maybe Trevor.

Seven people had liked the post. One of them was flexed-muscle guy, D-Man. Small world. D-Man had also liked the news reposting and the release-date article. In fact, he'd liked all of Keith's posts for months. I finally got tired of checking the posts. D-

Man had commented a few times as well. He used that same hashtag, #StayFlexed, and the same misspelling of "gruvy" as he did on my public page posts. I wasn't sure if it was by choice. Maybe it was some version of ironic that younger people found cool. Either way, I kinda liked that D-Man dug the word "groovy." It possibly showed an appreciation for the hippies of the sixties that I found odd given his #StayFlexed attitude.

The news story was the one about Keith being presumed dead and the search for his body ending. The video of his fall played again. It froze before the final plunge and was replaced by Keith's smiling photo. "Keith Dalton, presumed dead at twenty-three years old."

Presumed dead.

A YouTube search yielded the video in its entirety. The camera seemed to be perched on the ground facing the river with the dock low in the frame. Keith stumbled into the shot, tripped, flew back, crossed his arm over his face and spun away from camera. I rewound it, played it again and froze the frame on Keith flying back with his arm over his face - cheated away from the camera. It was a stunt fall.

My head spun. A stunt fall? Was he self-taping an audition when something went wrong? That could explain why there was no one behind the camera. It might explain why he felt the need to do it at night when no one was around. It began to seem reasonable that Keith was his own witness.

Assuming it was Keith. With only his abandoned phone to identify his body, it was possible someone else was doing the stunt. Maybe Keith was filming it for a friend and ran away when it went wrong. No, he would've instinctively run into the shot looking for his friend. I'd already worked that out. No, it was either Keith, or Keith was a psychopathic mastermind who'd premeditated the entire thing and faked his own death. That seemed unlikely. Keith was dead. That made sense.

The article about the movie release date didn't seem special. D-Man had liked it, of course. I scrolled down to older posts again and read a few. Mostly workout tips and mundane observations about waiting in line, procrastinating and cleaning. My eyes locked on the post about Gravity A playing a bar in Mid-City. "Check out this gruvy band."

My fingers slashed the mousepad, scrolling rapidly until I found a post about Bar Tonique on Rampart. "Check out this gruvy bar."

What were the odds that Keith Dalton and D-Man would both have an appreciation for the hippies of the sixties and a #StayFlexed attitude? What were the odds they'd use the same misspelling? Actually, those odds could be fairly high. Social media had exposed the shortcomings of our education system many times in many ways.

D-Man's "about" page was blank save revealing he lived in New Orleans. He still only had a few dozen friends though he'd joined Facebook in 2008. Keith hadn't joined until early 2009 but D-Man had "liked" him from the start. It kinda made me feel better that D-Man had joined before Keith. It helped close the open question left by the missing body. It seemed less likely they were the same guy if D-Man's page predated Keith's. Besides, why would Keith fake his own death and stalk Bryan? It didn't make sense.

Without a photo of his face, a phone number or an address, it seemed beyond my grasp to even try to figure out D-Man's real name. There wasn't much to click. His photos were all memes. There was no birthday. Maybe the friends held clues. The first was a bodybuilder from Minneapolis, Colt Seavers. Sounded like something from a soap opera. He'd joined Facebook in 2008 and had about sixty friends. Cameron Railsback was a young, handsome stunt guy in L.A. with dozens of friends. Nina Franklin was a pretty brunette who said she was an actor. That would be easy enough to check. Among her hundreds of friends were Keith Dalton and Cameron Railsback.

Jody Banks worked at a shop in L.A. A beautiful blonde in her twenties, she had over 400 friends and posted lots of selfies, all liked by D-Man. And Cameron Railsback. And Colt Seavers. And Nina Franklin. Hmmm.

I opened two browser windows, comparing the names of the people who'd liked Jodi's latest selfie with the list of D-Man's friends. Sonny Hooper and Gwen Doyle also overlapped. Sonny was a mechanic in New Orleans and Gwen Doyle was a girl-next-door from St. Paul. That seemed like an unusual group of people to have in common.

Sonny didn't post much but most of his posts were liked by D-Man, Colt, Cameron, Jody, Nina, Sonny and Gwen. The older posts were also liked by Keith Dalton. When I was checking Gwen's likes, the words jumped at me like a neon sign, "Check out this gruvy movie. Hey, I rhymed!" Why would Gwen misspell groovy the same way D-Man and Keith did?

I dragged one of Gwen's photos to a reverse image search and held my breath. The photo was from a Twitter account for Mindy Sessions. I didn't have Twitter so I looked her up on Facebook. Boom. Mindy was a cheerleader at UConn with a fiancée, family members and links to former employers. Seemed pretty legit. Maybe Gwen was "catfishing" Mindy, stealing her photos to create an online identity.

I hadn't gone to Sundance this year but everyone who'd seen the documentary, *Catfish,* said it was amazing. I was thrilled when a friend sent me a screener. What started as an internet love story turned into a story of how blind love made us, how much we all wanted to be loved and what a deceptive escape the internet could be.

The term "catfish" was something the catfisher's husband had come up with when he was describing his compassion for his wife's alternate universe. He said one time there were these fish they were trying to ship across the ocean but their skin would get mushy from sitting dormant. Someone put a catfish in the tank and it kept all the other fish active. The husband said there were people who did that - they kept people thinking. He seemed to think it was a good thing - a healthy-skinned fish thing.

A Google search of Gwen Doyle gave too many options and none were in St. Paul, Minnesota.

Minnesota. Wasn't that where Keith was from?

An image search of semi-rugged Sonny Hooper's photo matched a model working in Texas, Logan

George. Possibly also a fake name, but I could see a model named George Logan switching things for dramatic effect. Logan George had a very longstanding and elaborate Facebook page with thousands of friends. Seemed legit. Sonny was catfishing Logan? What were the odds on going two-for-two finding false online identities?

I pressed my luck and searched a photo of the dashing Colt Seavers. Zach Tosch, a fitness model featured in dozens of bodybuilding magazines, popped up. He didn't have a Facebook page, and I still didn't have Twitter. Colt was catfishing Zach? The odds were becoming fantastic so I tried a search of Colt's name. Without any other specifics, all that came up was the Lee Majors character in *The Fall Guy*. I used to love that show. I added Minnesota and found one more thread to pull, but it was just an avatar name for someone who used to post on a hockey forum. There was an email but it made no sense to try it. I was beginning to feel a bit like I was spying, invading privacy, but I told myself that as long as I wasn't paying for the information, I was just "looking things up."

Nina Franklin's name was too common to find a clue. Her photos came from the account of an ingenue in L.A. who'd apparently just booked her first commercial. I remembered those days. I couldn't find Cameron Railsback's photos. A Google search of Cameron's name brought up an entire page of links to the movie *The Stunt Man*. I'd liked that one. Steve Railsback played Cameron (no last name), a fugitive who hides out on a set pretending to be a stunt man. Barbara Hershey played Cameron's love interest...

Nina Franklin. My heart was pounding. I was onto something.

I didn't even bother with Jody Banks' photo. It was sure to be a fake. I jumped straight to her name. Images of Heather Thomas in a bikini spanned the search page. Jody Banks was the resourceful babe from *The Fall Guy* - a TV show about a stunt man. I was definitely onto something. These weren't coincidences, these were clues.

I searched Sonny Hooper's name and found Burt Reynolds as *Hooper*, "The Greatest Stuntman Alive."

I ran Keith's photo just for safe measure. Totally legit. Keith was real. Presumed dead, but real.

D-Man would remain a mystery. Other than Keith, he was the only one who hadn't used a fake photo but a cartoon, flexed arm wasn't much to go on. I ran it through the image search anyway, of course, but found nothing.

I stopped to think. Almost everyone in this mutual admiration society of "likers" appeared to have gotten their photos from unsuspecting people. At least three of them had used the "gruvy" misspelling. Everyone had D-Man in common. He seemed to be at the center of things. All of them had created their accounts in the last two years or so. What if they were all D-Man? Except Keith. Keith was Keith. And Keith was dead. Presumed dead. They never found a body.

What if Keith was D-Man? He created the D-Man account first? That didn't seem to make sense. Why would someone create an anonymous account before they'd created a real one? Why would I?

I was reluctant to open a Facebook page. Sofia

and my blog had pressured me into it. My anonymous blog. Why had I made my blog anonymous? Fear of failure? Fear of being critiqued? Fear of associating one part of my life to another? Fear of stalkers being able to track me? I had to admit they were thoughts I'd had when I was deciding.

When I thought about it that way, I could see starting a page to express views I was afraid to own, but D-Man wasn't opinionated about anything particularly contentious. Scrolling his posts again, it hit me that most of his likes were actually from himself. He was guaranteeing himself approval and web activity. A "social media presence" was fast becoming a deciding factor in casting. What if he'd created D-Man and the gang to praise Keith as he was starting his career? What if Keith created D-Man and the gang to praise himself as he was starting his career? That actually made sense. It seemed extraordinarily elaborate, but it made sense. Faking a death seemed extraordinarily elaborate as well, but it was beginning to sound less left-field than it had an hour before.

If D-Man was Keith, then he was still alive and "liking." I went back to Bryan's page and scanned his posts again. His posts were liked by dozens, even hundreds of people, but D-Man's personalities were often among them. Jody commented that the most recent photo of Bryan and Trevor was "gruvy." That made at least four personalities using "gruvy." I began checking all the comments for more uses of the misspelled word. Though I was coming up empty, I did notice that their comments were mostly reserved for photos with Trevor.

Checking the likes and comments on Trevor's page, I found some of same band of imposters. Gwen thought Trevor's flexed-arm photo was "gruvy." If I hadn't already ruled him out, I might've thought the cartoon was based on Trevor's flexed arm and wondered if he was D-Man. No, Trevor was a real person like Keith and I'd accounted for his whereabouts. A quick check of Trevor's friends showed he wasn't friends with Keith, though a few in the D-Man clan had managed to connect.

What if D-Man wasn't stalking Bryan? What if he was stalking Trevor? The stuntman. That actually made more sense. The photo the stalker had given the postman was of both Bryan and Trevor at the door of the shop. We were getting ready to shoot Trevor's stunt when the hoodie-guy appeared behind the set's bushes. The missing journal was a gift from Trevor with his signed inscription. Perhaps the stalker was jealous. Maybe that explained his interest in following me after I'd gone to the shop.

I texted Trevor, asking him to meet me for coffee at 11:30. Then I called Bryan. "Hey, it's Charlotte."

"Charlotte, what a pleasant surprise." His voice was welcoming.

"Can you meet for a coffee tomorrow? I think I may have figured out what's going on."

"With the stalker?"

"Yes."

"Do tell. I hate suspense."

"I need to double-check everything, but I think you may be in the clear."

"You found him?"

"I'm still puzzling it out. Let me look at it all

again and I'll tell you everything tomorrow."

"I'll look forward to it... if I must."

I laughed. "Patience is a virtue. Noon at Rue de la Course on Magazine."

"See you there."

I spent the better part of the night scanning posts for more clues and writing charts with lines connecting everyone. As it all lined up, I was feeling pretty gruvy.

Chapter 20

I'd always been one of those "better to have it and not need it than need it and not have it" people, but I was also a fan of packing light. I brought some of the notes I'd written but left my laptop at home. The coffee shop was fairly empty. Trevor came in behind me as I was scanning for a table with privacy. "Hey!"

"Hey!" He hugged me and we lined up at the counter. "Bryan's not here yet?"

"I told him to come at noon. I had a few questions I was hoping you could help me answer."

"I'll try." He smiled at the young barista. "Espresso. And she'll have..."

"Mint Green Tea. Medium."

We paid and took our number to the corner table furthest from the door. Trevor settled into the booth then lightly slapped his thighs. "Hit me. What do you want to know?"

"Did you know Keith Dalton?"

"The kid that drowned? Yeah. He was on a couple of me and Bryan's movies. Why?"

"Did you know him well?"

"Not really. I helped him with a few things he was working on. He wanted to be a stuntman so I gave him a few pointers."

"On set?"

Trevor was getting restless. "Yeah, base camp.

Charlotte, why are you asking me this?"

"Did you talk to him about how to do that water fall you did in our movie?"

"Yeah, actually. He 'd heard about the movie and asked me to help him."

"Then you got the job?"

"Well, yeah. I pretty much had the job the minute Bryan got the lead."

My mind went into hyperdrive. Finally, there was a window into the thing every actor needed to make a character work - a motive. Was Keith angry at Trevor for taking his job? Did he feel betrayed? He'd brought the job to Trevor's attention and might've thought he'd stolen it. Was he angry at Bryan? If Bryan hadn't gotten the part, maybe Keith would've had a shot. At least in his mind. "When did you get that job? The one we did."

"Awhile ago. They offered the part to Bryan while they were getting their financing together. It was only a few days after Keith had asked for help."

The beverages arrived. Neither of us got up to add sugar or cream.

"Charlotte, seriously, why are you asking all this about Keith?"

I wanted to understand more before I attempted explaining it to someone else. "I know. I'm sorry. Can I just ask one more thing? I'm trying to understand this. So, Keith knew about the movie before you did?"

"He said he'd heard about it at the gym. There were some guys talking about making a movie here and Keith had some fantasy that he was going to somehow get a stunt gig on it."

"And it was a fantasy because he had no experience?"

"No experience, no credentials, no resume and no connections."

"He didn't know any stunt coordinators?"

"He barely knew me, and I'm just a guy lookin' for a gig. I can't say I woulda vouched for him, though. He came on a little strong, you know what I mean?"

"No. Strong, how? Like coming on to you?"

"Just really eager, you know? He never tried to find an excuse to touch me or anything, nothing like that. He just kept bugging me about helping him."

"He wanted you to break him into the business or he just wanted to spend more time with you?"

He adjusted his weight on his seat. "It was more like he wanted me to be impressed, like he had something to prove. He'd say things like, 'I'm going to be the biggest stuntman ever,' or 'I'm going to be the most famous whatever, you'll see' like he had something to prove. Only I never said anything particularly discouraging so it always seemed weird that he wanted me to see."

"But you don't think maybe he had a crush on you?"

"Oh, he definitely had a crush on me. I mean, maybe just a bro-crush but he'd bring me gifts for helping him, want to hang out after work, stuff like that."

"Gifts?"

"Nothing big. A couple times he brought me an espresso because he knew I liked them and they didn't have a machine on set."

"Is there anything else?"

"Not really. Maybe if you told me what this is about I could be more helpful." He smiled and batted his lashes.

"I know. I'm so sorry. Okay, I just want to say it all out loud. So, Keith came to you for help about the water stunt because he'd heard there was a movie getting ready to shoot here."

"Yeah, but that wasn't the first time. He'd been asking for help since I met him on the movie before."

"And you'd give him pointers, then he would try and impress you." I pushed my straw down and it made that weird plastic-on-plastic noise.

"Yeah. Sometimes he'd show me something at work. A couple times he asked me to look at videos."

"Wait, what?"

"He'd make these videos and ask me to watch them. Look, the kid needed a lot of encouragement and I tried to give it to him but he was insatiable, you know? He needed to hear he was going to be famous. I kept trying to tell him there's no such thing as a famous stuntman."

"Zoe Bell."

"Yeah, but not really until after she played a part as an actor. Then it all came together. The point is, stunts aren't a clear path to fame. You don't chose a job that, when done well, is designed to give someone else the credit if what you want is to be on TMZ."

"Good golly, is that how we measure fame now? Yikes."

He laughed. "Just sayin'."

I snapped back to task. "But, wait. The videos."

"Of stunts. Stuff he needed props for or like a rooftop fall. That kind of thing."

"Like if he'd wanted to do a water fall, he woulda needed water."

"A pool."

"Or a river."

Trevor's face lost it's warmth. "Tell me what's going on."

"What if Keith was shooting the water stunt for you when he fell into the river?"

Trevor said nothing. His eyes blinked a little. "I'd be lying if I said it never crossed my mind."

"But you never said anything."

"Like what? It was ruled an accident. Nothing I had to say would've changed that. Bottom line, I had no idea what happened. I barely knew the guy."

"You weren't even friends on Facebook."

"He sent me a request but I ignored it. I thought he'd be one of those aggressive types who think it's cool to post things on your page."

"Do you know D-Man on Facebook? I mean, is he a friend of yours in life?"

"Demon?"

"D-Man. He's a friend of yours on Facebook. He has an icon with a flexed arm?"

"That guy." He chuckled. "Yeah. I mean, no, I never met the guy but he's always liking my posts, saying how cool it must be to work with famous people, stuff like that."

Bryan waved from the door and ordered at the counter.

I turned back to Trevor. "Has D-Man ever seemed to know something about you he shouldn't have known, something personal or something you hadn't shared on Facebook?"

Trevor's mouth dropped open. "There was one time he wished me a happy birthday."

"It's not on your Facebook account? What about IMDb?"

"Luckily, they haven't gotten me yet. Those guys are ruthless."

"Preach. So, there's nowhere he could've found your birthday online without paying for it?"

"No. Well, everyone at work on that first movie knew. We were shooting then and the director gave me a cake. The crew sang and everything."

"The crew - meaning Keith was there?"

Bryan greeted us both and sat next to Trevor. "What did I miss?"

I pulled the notes from my crocheted backpack. "I think I may have figured it out."

"You know who's stalking me?" Bryan looked at Trevor. "Do you know?"

I unfolded the list of Facebook names. "I'm pretty sure I know who's doing the stalking, but I'm also pretty sure you're not being stalked."

Bryan looked confused.

"I think the stalker is after Trevor, not you."

"Really?" Taken aback, Bryan's chin lifted. "Well, that's a wrinkle."

I explained about Keith Dalton being on two of their movies. Trevor filled in the details about Keith wanting to be a stuntman, about how he'd helped him with pointers.

I jumped in. "Yes, his obituary actually said that he'd gone to New Orleans to pursue his dream of being a stuntman."

Bryan sounded cautious, "Okay."

"I think that he may have been making a video of a stunt when he disappeared."

Trevor clarified, "He used to show me videos to impress me and try to get me to help him break into the business."

"Did he have a crush on you?"

Trevor guffawed. "Why does everyone think that?"

I laughed. "Dude, you look like Superman's hotter brother. Everyone has a crush on you."

Bryan laughed too. "I take solace in knowing people think you can double me."

"Okay, okay. I'm cute."

I waved my arms. "No. Dude, you're gorgeous. It's indisputable. But that's not the point. Okay, so Keith goes missing."

"He died, didn't he?" Bryan was suddenly serious.

"Presumed dead. They never found a body."

Bryan was quiet a minute. "He let his family hold a funeral for him? Who would do such a thing?"

It did sound a little crazy. "Maybe someone who wanted to be famous. Maybe someone who wanted the world to see he could've done that stunt." I figured Bryan had known his fair share of fame-seekers.

"So you think the stalker is Keith? Why? How?"

"I'm not sure if he meant for everyone to think he was dead. Maybe he had trouble getting out of the water. Maybe he drifted too far to retrieve the phone before someone found it. Maybe it wasn't premeditated. Maybe he just liked the attention and went with it."

"Wow." Trevor was in.

Bryan remained unconvinced. "Then he became a stalker?"

"Apparently, he always wanted Trevor's approval. He wanted to prove he could be a famous stuntman. And, as we've already established, he may've had a crush on Trevor. I can't think of any other reason to take the journal."

"The journal?" Trevor took a breath. "I have a confession." He lowered his head, shook it, then faced Bryan. "That was a regift."

"You gave me a regifted journal?"

"I know. I..."

I tapped the table. "That's not the point. Who gave you the journal, Trevor?"

"I told you he gave me gifts sometimes. But honestly, I'm not the journaling type."

Bryan didn't like being left out. "Who gave you gifts?"

I looked at Trevor and answered, "Keith."

"Yes."

Bryan tried to catch up. "The drowned kid gave you that journal? And you regifted it to me?"

I laughed. "Bryan, forget about the regifting. The point is Keith is the only other person we know of with a connection to that journal."

Trevor jumped in. "But why send us the photo at the store?"

"Maybe he wanted the attention. Maybe he got tired of playing dead. Maybe he wanted to scare you away from Trevor, let you know he was watching."

Bryan was still skeptical. "This all seems a bit

dramatic. Doesn't it make more sense that this Keith kid is dead and someone else is doing all of this?"

I smoothed the list of names and pushed it to the middle of the table. Neither of them had heard of *Catfish* so I explained about creating fake profiles to lure people. I pointed out the fake names, how they were all Facebook friends who liked and shared Keith's and D-Man's posts. I explained that they'd used other people's photos as their own to create their profiles, that many of them had used the same misspelling of "gruvy" and that their names were from movies and TV shows about stuntmen.

Trevor looked up from the page full of connecting lines and green highlights indicating "gruvy" people. "So, they're all D-Man?"

"It would appear."

Bryan clarified, "And D-Man is the catfish name for Keith."

"I'm just guessing. But I do think it's a good guess."

Bryan seemed satisfied. "So, what now?"

I wasn't entirely sure. I'd honestly never thought past figuring out the puzzle. "I'm thinking Trevor should call the police. You can take this chart with you if you want. You should probably tell them to take his computer if they arrest him for anything."

Trevor shook his head. "They're not going to care about a stalker."

"Probably not, but the kid faked his death and cost this city money lookin' for 'im. My guess is they'd like to know who did that."

Bryan's voice was firm. "She's right, Trevor. And if he's alive, his family should know."

211

Trevor looked at his hands. "I guess."

I piled on reasons. "He could've broken a lot of laws. There may have been a life insurance policy. He could've left debt."

Trevor sighed. "He was definitely in debt."

I continued. "He could've started a new identity with a stolen social security number. Who knows? You have to tell someone."

"Dang." He picked up his phone. "Will you stay while I call? They'll probably have questions and you seem to have all the answers."

"Of course."

The police were confused at first but promised to send someone out. Bryan had to leave before they arrived. He extended his arms and I rose to hug him. He whispered, "Thank you."

I pulled back and looked at him. "Hopefully this is the end of it."

We hugged again and said goodbye before Trevor and I settled in to wait for the police.

Trevor was still processing. "Why? I mean, it makes sense that he was making a video of the water stunt and the whole missing-kid thing wasn't planned. I get that. And I can see why he might blame me for taking that job if he's not thinking straight. So the photo was to scare me?"

I stirred the last of my tea with the straw. "I don't know, but for sure he wanted you to know he was watching. Like a jealous lover? Or like a fan?"

He laughed. "More like paparazzi."

"True dat."

"So, what's with the journal?"

"If he saw you guys as friends or more, I'm sure

he was hurt by you giving away his gift. We already know he was watching you, and it's possible he was the guy behind the bushes on set, so he might've been watching when you went into the trailer with it and came out empty-handed."

"Yeah, okay. Creepy." He shivered.

"I know, right? So if he imagined some type of deeper relationship, he might've been jealous and wanted it back. Or maybe he wanted it because you'd written something in it."

"Creepier still."

"Yeah but that's kinda normal stalker stuff. I have a lot of friends in the business and it's kind of a defining characteristic of a stalker - they imagine some deeper relationship and look for, like secret messages from you."

"Secret messages?"

"Yeah, like you post on Facebook something like, 'Great day on set hangin' with friends,' and Keith thinks you're talking to him about him. Specifically."

"Jeeze."

"Price o' fame, man."

Trevor laughed.

"Actually, stalking is mostly not for celebrities but when it is, it's often the lesser known people because they seem more accessible. I've had a few - starting long before I became an actor. Tell you the truth, after I saw that hoodie-guy behind my fence, I freaked out a little."

"So, what was that about? Why would Keith be behind your fence?"

I sipped the last of my tea. "Assuming it was the same guy, I think he followed us home after we came to the shop. Don't you think he was watching the shop that day to see what happened when you got the photo from the postman? I think he saw us in there for a long time talking to you guys, and he probably knew who I was and that we worked together. I hate to keep bangin' this drum but I think he thought y'all were BFF's or lovers or something."

"You don't think he was just angry about the job he didn't get?"

"As an actor, I just gotta say it's not as strong a choice. It doesn't answer as many questions and that story has holes. Jealousy makes everything make some kinda sense."

Trevor nodded his head slowly. "Makes me feel weird about helping him."

"Yeah, but don't let it shut you down. I'd rather be nice to people and be wrong than be mean and be wrong."

Officer Landry arrived and took Trevor's statement. He seemed unimpressed at first. I explained that D-Man appeared to be Keith. I told him about D-Man's fake profile and all the people writing "gruvy." I called it a "virtual handwriting match" to sound more legit. I listed possible charges associated with faking an identity then closed, "Bottom line, if Keith is alive, he used city resources for days on end and should be called to account for it."

We all walked out together and Officer Landry handed us cards. "Call me if you hear from him again." He seemed intrigued and that would have to be enough.

Trevor hugged me and started to walk away. "See

you on set sometime."

"Till our paths cross again."

Magazine Street was fairly busy with tourists and shoppers. Albert wasn't around. Must've been eating or walking. I window-shopped Fleurty Girl then saw the bench in front of the Sabai jewelry shop covered with feather boas and fresh flowers. Someone local had clearly passed and a memorial was growing. I stopped to look at the notice in the window. There were two photos printed onto the paper, an old photo of a young, handsome man in a military uniform and beside it, a photo of Albert with his salt-and-pepper dreads and milky eye. I felt all the air go out of me. A tear rolled involuntarily. The notice said they were raising funds for a second line in his honor.

I looked back to the memorial. There were toys and a xylophone. Wooden letters spelled out "FAMILY." Many people had left notes. One read, "If all of us bring just half the sunshine to the day Albert did, it is a life well lived." Another ended with, "And thank you for getting me across the street when I was drunk." I chuckled. Then stopped. Dang.

I walked home in a daze. Albert and I didn't know each other well, but I had genuine love for him and felt his for me. Apparently, everyone did. The notice had called him the "Moses of Magazine Street" who always had a blessing for everyone.

It was hard to rally when it came time for the humid walk to the free Wednesday at the Square concert. I contemplated missing it altogether. With movies, if you missed a showing, there would be another one, but concerts were ephemeral. Either you were there or you weren't. Albert was reminding me that any day could be my last.

Wednesday at the Square was one of the many events where the proceeds benefitted a local non-profit. I loved how just buying a cold beer was a way of giving back. It made me feel good about spending money.

I settled near the front of the stage behind somebody's Paw Paw in a psychedelic shirt with an image of Jimmy Hendrix staring from his back. Billy Iuso & the Restless Natives opened the show. At some point, Iuso invited his eight year old daughter, Aria, to join him onstage and sing along. She was adorable but what struck me was how brave she was standing on that stage with a giant microphone in her little face and a big crowd stretched out before her. A breeze blew her wispy hair around making her seem angelic. I loved watching Iuso passing his culture and heritage to his daughter. Maybe she'd grow up to be a scientist or a teacher or whatever, but she'd be ready for it. Being brave at eight was normal for her.

The Junco Partners came on next and played originals and covers while we all sang, danced and swayed, sticky with humidity. Dancing Man 504 jumped high into the air closer to the stage. He danced his way through the crowd, stopping at times to dance with people in the crowd. The rippled, rich skin on his six-pack was slick with sweat. He danced his way toward me with the fancy footwork of second line parades. We danced together for the last song. As we applauded the band, he leaned into me, "You goin'a Rebirth?"

"Rebirth's playin'? Where?"

"Bourbon."

I was surprised Rebirth Brass Band would play anywhere on Bourbon Street. Those venues tended to feature cover bands playing pop and rock favorites. "Which club?"

"On the street."

The clapping stopped and the crowd started to disperse.

"You're saying Rebirth is playing on the actual street?"

"Wanna walk with me? Come on."

Though we'd taken it over during the Super Bowl, most locals didn't frequent Bourbon Street. New Orleanians could be downright snotty about mixing with the drunk and disorderly tourist crowd on Bourbon. But local Louisianans came to Bourbon Street year round, and I wouldn't necessarily have called someone from Baton Rouge or Slidell a tourist. As a teenager, I would drive forty minutes from my home in Maryland to Georgetown, D.C. to hang out all the time. It never occurred to me that I would be called a tourist there. I'd been going to Bourbon with my cousins for decades and had a lot of memories of good times there. I wasn't ready to be snotty about how fun it could be to hang out on Bourbon.

Dancing Man 504 turned out to be Darryl. He was in his forties but was a sinewy, buff, bundle of energy. We laughed about both having bodies that fooled people about our age. Then laughed again about him having the advantage of more melanin to fight wrinkles.

A flatbed was parked in front of Rita's Tequila House where they were having a block party to celebrate Cinco de Mayo. "Hot" girls carried big trays of tequila shots for sale. The band was getting ready inside the neon-lit bar. Darryl was greeting the guys in the band when Derrick's eyes locked with mine. "Hey!"

We hugged and I told him how excited I was to see them play again. He seemed so humble, like it was no big deal to see this amazing band in concert - for free. In the street. I'd first heard Rebirth in movies like *The Skeleton Key* and *Boomerang*. And there was that YouTube video of them playing *Do Watcha Wanna* while second-lining through the French Quarter. I'd watched it dozens of times when I lived in L.A. and it always calmed me, made me joyful. For me, the Rebirth guys were more than musicians, they were healers.

The sparse crowd outside was mostly locals who knew what a rare treat this was. The tourists walked past with mild interest.

I tapped dancing Darryl. "Where are they headed that would be better than this?"

"They have no idea what they're listenin' to. They lookin' for someone playin' music they know."

The band passed a plastic bucket to collect dollars. Most of the crowd didn't contribute. It was getting easier to see why the guys in the band were so humble. We were so spoiled for music here that it was hard to remember how special and rare it all was. I'd all but stopped going to movie theatres, opting instead to soak in all the live music I could manage. It felt a little like being a kid who finds a new best friend and starts ignoring the old one. I was fiercely loyal and movies had always been there for me, but so had music and now it was as alive as the actors I'd surrounded myself with in L.A.

Dancing with abandon as tourists wandered past, I felt love and joy bubble up in me. Dang it, another happy-cry. It was becoming a regular, semi-embarrassing occurrence. Tears streamed, hips moved, curls swayed and I felt electric.

Chapter 21

It was another humid day but I walked to the store for groceries. I instinctively looked to the table and chair in front of Design Within Reach, but Albert wasn't there. His memorial was getting more elaborate. The flowers were dying and the balloons had deflated, but the offerings were piling up. I especially liked the photos of Albert with neighborhood children.

The local news was on when I got home and started unpacking the bags. The latest Wile E. Coyote attempt at containing the flow of BP oil had failed. No surprise. The incessant images of explosions had been replaced by images of burning water and oil-covered birds. Tar balls were washing up on Dauphine Island in Alabama. The fishing ban had been extended. Families who'd lived off the land for generations feared for their entire way of life. It was clear the worst was yet to come.

The jerk from BP was saying how they'd "make us whole." I was pretty sure there wouldn't be a box on their form for "lost my entire culture and ability to sustain myself." And, of course there'd be no box for "got dumped by my boyfriend." I put away groceries and tried to ignore the horrors unfolding on the TV. As I turned back to empty the last of the bags, I caught Keith Dalton's face onscreen. I dropped a

Zapp's potato chips bag and ran to pause the program. Keith's photo stared out. I rewound to the beginning of the story.

"You may remember Keith Dalton as the young man from Minnesota who disappeared into the Mississippi River last March, as seen in this video."

It all seemed so obvious now that the mystery had unraveled. It was clearly a video of Keith doing the same stunt Trevor had done in our movie.

"Dalton's disappearance resulted in an exhaustive search. After expending city resources for days, Dalton was presumed dead."

The next video over the newscaster's shoulder was of Keith being walked out of a building in handcuffs. "Using a 'digital handwriting' match and fake Facebook profiles, police were able to track down Dalton in this Lower Garden District hostel where he'd been living since shortly after his disappearance. Fellow residents were shocked."

A twenty-something stood in front of a nearby coffee shop wearing an apron. "He'd come in here. I waited on him sometimes. He had the brown hair and brown eyes though. Didn't look like the picture of the kid. And he usually wore a hoodie. He seemed okay. Never really thought about him much one way or the other."

A regular customer remarked, "He was one of those kind of people that you don't really notice, you know?"

There was some irony in Keith being famous for not being memorable.

The newscaster popped back onto the screen. "In a Hollywood South twist, Dalton was arrested for trespassing and stalking after it was discovered that he'd been following a former coworker who was helping him break into the biz. Dalton may also face charges of insurance fraud in his home state. City officials expressed anger that Dalton exploited the city's emergency resources in their prolonged search."

I rewound the story and watched them walk Keith out in handcuffs again. I froze it as he peeked out from under his grey hoodie. "Gotcha."

It felt pretty good to know I'd helped expose the charade, answer the riddle of his faked death and put an end to his hunting. My phone rang. Bryan. "You saw?"

"It was on when I came in the door and turned on the TV. Wild, right?"

"I'm just glad it's over. I know he wasn't really after me, but I thought he was. In a way, Trevor was spared that."

I hadn't really thought about that. "He was stressed out for you. So was I. Heck, even my mom and niece ask about you when they call."

"Tell them I say hello, will you? That's so kind of them. I'm at the store and Trevor's looking for someone to go to the Prytania with him tonight to celebrate. Can I tell him you'll join him? I'm going to have to decline."

I could hear Trevor in the background. "Say yes!"

"Sure. What's playing?"

Trevor grabbed the phone. "*Iron Man 2*. You down?"

I was.

There was a line outside the theatre and as people streamed into the building, I spotted the tall, handsome man from the streetcar and a jolt ran up my spine. I kept my eye out for him as we found seats in the crowded theatre. He was getting up from a chair a few rows behind us as we settled in. As the lights went down and the singing, animated soda sang, he sat down next to the kind of bombshell you'd find tattooed onto a sailor's bicep and handed her a soda. As she stood to take off her leather biker jacket, her curves burst through her clingy tank top revealing she had tattoos of her own.

I turned back to the screen hoping Trevor hadn't noticed. If that was the kind of woman Tall Guy liked, I was definitely not his type. My days of competing with hotties were behind me. And her curves were all original parts. My long, slender lines were no match for a natural-born brick house. Plus, she seemed like a "bad girl." I was more the front-row, straight-A-student type.

Iron Man swept me up into another world until we were leaving the theatre and I noticed myself trying to spot Tall Guy on our way out. With no luck.

As we hugged goodbye, Trevor thanked me again for helping and I thanked him for making me celebrate our win.

My phone rang as I walked into the house. "Hey Taffy, what's goin' on?"

"I heard from Lillibette that you solved another mystery. You should be a detective."

I laughed. "I'd rather play it on TV. But I do want to solve my family mystery. Yours too."

"That's why I'm calling. Sit Jojo. Sit. Sit. Good boy. I talked to Chiffon and I even got UncaParis to fill in a few things. He said Mama Heck said it was the owner's wife what named Eunoe."

"That explains how a slave might get a name from Greek mythology or Dante. But how did Eunoe know to name her child Hecuba?"

"Oh, UncaParis said that's for sure Mama Heck's name. I think he felt bad we didn't already know. He said they was named for the *Iliad*. Guessed we didn't know since Mama named us different."

"What did Chiffon say?"

"Somebody come walk this dog! Why's it always gotta be me walks this dog? Come on, Jojo. He's so cute now, Charlotte. You gotta see him. I'll put a picture on Facebook."

"Oh yay. I'll look for it. So, Chiffon?"

"Yeah, so Chiffon say remember how Mama Heck always talked about the breadcrumbs? Mama Heck used to say names was breadcrumbs leadin' you back to yourself. Said they're a trail to your history. I never paid much mind since we was basket kids. But you the one what showed me our names was breadcrumbs too. I'm thinkin' you can figure this out."

"Do you know her birthday?"

"Mama Eunoe? I doubt anyone knows. Might be on her grave marker, I guess."

"Where's she resting?"

"Lord knows. Maybe UncaParis. I'll ask him next time I talk to him if he seems in the mood. Why does it matter?"

"It's just an idea. That Dante story with the Eunoe river that strengthens your memory of your good deeds, it has dates. The soul goes to the river at noon on Wednesday, March thirtieth, their Easter. There was another date other people think it might be. I forget but it was in April. Either way, she'd be an Aries, if that matters."

"There you go, makin' sense again. You got this. Wait, that's Chiffon. I'ma put her on. Gimme a minute."

I searched my computer for the "Cassandra" file and reviewed some of my research.

Taffy interrupted me. "Charlotte?"

"Hey."

"Chiffon, you on?"

"Hey! I'm here."

"Tell her what you told me about the breadcrumbs. Jojo, leave that alone. Drop it."

Chiffon snickered. "Got your hands full with that pup. He's so cute. Have you seen him, Charlotte?"

I laughed. "Yeah, I'll look at the new photos right after this call."

"Okay, so Mama Heck and Mama both would tell us about how names were breadcrumbs that would lead you back to yourself, to your heritage."

"Did they use that word, 'heritage?'"

"Yeah. I always loved that word."

Taffy interjected. "I hated it, sounded like somethin' I was never gonna have. But, I've been thinkin' 'bout what you said, Charlotte, 'bout how heritage is the culture and ideas your family passes to you. I don't have her genes but I got Mama's culture and ideas. Heck, just this week, I taught my six year old 'bout the rules of football while he's sittin' there in a Saints jersey I bought him. And my eight year old helped me with the dirty rice tonight. I got all that from Mama."

Chiffon laughed. "You made dirty rice tonight? I made dirty rice tonight!"

I guessed this happened a lot with them. "That's crazy. I'm glad you're feelin' better about it all, Taffy."

"Both of us," Chiffon added. "But, listen, I remembered something. Mama and Mama Heck got in a round-and-round once about our names, mine and Taffy's. Mama Heck was sayin' the same old thing about names bein' a breadcrumb trail you leave for your children's children. Mama said she was doing that and that Mama Heck oughta leave it be."

Taffy prodded. "Yeah, but tell 'er what happened next."

"So, Mama says that Mama Heck had always said, if you don't know your heritage, create one. Mama Heck said that was passed from slave days when families would be sold from each other."

"Wow." I always felt so small and confused in the face of man's inhumanity to man.

"So, Mama says if it was good enough for our mothers' mothers, it's good enough for her babies. That her babies had two paths to follow and they had a right. Then Mama Heck took her hand and said that Mama had done good by us. She basically said Mama was right. Wouldn't't've believed it if I hadn't seen it with my own eyes."

"And you're just now remembering this?

Chiffon laughed. "No. I remembered it after you gave us the photo of our birth mother. We both remembered a bunch of things after that. I just didn't think it mattered anymore."

I chuckled. "Yeah, I get that."

Taffy jumped in. "But, she's still on the case. This

is that other path. We followed the Taffy and Chiffon breadcrumbs. Well, Charlotte did. Now, we're followin' the Cassandra path to our heritage. I love it."

"Yeah, Charlotte. We both really appreciate all you been doin' for us."

"I actually love doin' it. I dig research. I'm geeky like that. If y'all remember anything else, let me know. Oh, and Chiffon, do you know the name of Mama Eunoe's mother? Or maybe Mama Eunoe's birthday or where she's buried."

"UncaParis probably knows but we might be able to find the name. Taffy, do you have the family Bible or do I? You have it, don't you?"

The chandelier rattled down the hall. Mama Heck was at it again.

"It's somewhere."

"Mama kept that list in there, the list of names."

I was confused. "Like a family tree?"

Taffy jumped in. "I'll find it. Can't be too many places."

"It's not a tree, it's just a list. But I think it's her family's names. Taffy'll find it."

After we hung up, I searched for Taffy's Facebook page then scrolled down to a shot of the puppy in the grass. Jojo looked right up into the camera with his sympathy-inducing Pryor eyes.

The Cassandra notes were still open. Why the *Iliad*? Why leave breadcrumbs that lead back to a name given by an owner? Wouldn't you want to disown that heritage? Or at least forget it? Why lead your children's children to their ancestor's owner? I supposed that would lead everyone back to the plantation's name if they were sold from each other.

It was common for slaves to carry their owner's last names. Wouldn't that have been enough? Why a Greek mythology? And why didn't Mama Eunoe chose names from Dante's story instead? Did she know her name was the nymph's name? Was she named for her March thirtieth or Easter birthday? Did she know both stories and choose her heritage? That would seem absurd except that it was clear Mama Eunoe named her child for the nymph's daughter, Hecuba. Either Eunoe was also named for the *Iliad* and knew that or she knew both stories, was named for the river and chose a new heritage. That made sense.

The chandelier made a new jolting noise. My body jolted as well. I jumped up and made my way down the long hallway to my bedroom door. I never knew what I was going to see when I'd turn on that light. The "click" echoed against the high ceiling as the room filled with light. The chandelier was swinging back and forth like someone had just given it a big push.

I was fine with sleeping on the couch.

Chapter 22

The church was filled with Albert's family and people he affected in our community. I filed into the standing room in the back and smiled at the people next to me. The Bishop sang much of his service. He told us of the importance of talking to strangers. "You never know who someone is."

I told people that all the time. Maybe it was because my dad had been a spy. Maybe it was because I'd met so many actors who were nothing like their characters. Maybe it was because, like so many people, I'd been so misjudged so often.

The Bishop said Albert wasn't much of a churchgoer and that they normally didn't host funerals for non-parishioners, "But every preacher dreams of doing a celebrity funeral."

The jam-packed church laughed.

"From where I'm standing, looking out at all the faces of the non-parishioners who have joined us today, it's clear that Albert had a huge impact on our community."

When I left Los Angeles, I had to let go of many of my goals. I had to change what I wanted. I was still struggling to let go of some things but the bigger problem was that I'd had trouble coming up with new goals. The only thing I was clear about was that I wanted to be happy. Standing in the back of that church surrounded by children and the elderly, rich and poor, people who'd known Albert his whole life and people who knew him only as I had, I realized I had a new goal. I wanted to earn my second line parade. I wanted to affect so many people in my community so positively that they would feel compelled to create an impromptu memorial for me and take up a collection to get me a band and a police escort for my second line. If I was ever going to be "famous," I wanted to be the kind of celebrity Albert was, best known for his kindness.

Albert may not have attended church often, but he spread God's love every day. I attended the Moses of Magazine Street Church every time I passed Albert on the street and received his blessings. Wiping tears and looking around, I counted myself among Moses' many parishioners.

I spotted a box of tissues on my way out of the church and grabbed one. A plush woman with warm eyes saw that I was struggling and smiled. I smiled back, fighting tears.

She opened her arms, "Come here, baby." She held me like a mother, like she could make the whole world okay with hugs.

Outside, the crowd gathered for the second line. There were members of a social aid and pleasure club along with a brass band and a beautiful blue Mardi Gras Indian. The band played *I'll Fly Away* low and slow. As our crowd rounded the corner onto Magazine Street, the tempo picked up and we all sang along. I was getting used to singing and dancing with strangers in public. The police had closed the street and shopkeepers, cashiers and waiters poured onto the sidewalks to pay their respects.

We stopped in front of the memorial at Sabai jewelry store and danced in the street, me pumping my Saints-colors umbrella in time with the music.

Someone brought tiny paper cups of wine out for a toast. Everyone threw them back like shots then tossed the cups in the air.

We stopped again in front of the Design Within Reach store. Flowers and a flyer about Albert were displayed on the table where he used to sit. I was glad I had the kept the tissue.

We danced some more, sang some more, then moved onto the Walgreens. Employees came out and danced on the brick wall where Albert used to sit.

The last stop was a house with a sign out front honoring Albert. I knew nothing about this part of Albert's routines, had no idea who the people dancing on the porch were or their relationship to Albert.

The band broke into *Casanova* and some of the women ran up onto the porch to dance and bounce. I loved that booty-shaking to a sexy song wasn't inappropriate at funerals here. Albert had a good life and died a peaceful death. It made sense to celebrate.

At the repass, I filled a plate with rice, pasta, salad, green beans and chicken. A group of shopkeepers I recognized from my errands sat together on a low stone wall. We talked about Albert, how we knew him, how we'd miss him. The crowd was thinning and women began picking up errant cups and plates. I was finishing the last of my plate when I spotted a tall guy alone at the dessert table. A jolt went through me. "Excuse me."

I jumped up and joined him, checking out the

bread pudding, cookies and pralines. "Have you tried any of these?"

The tall guy turned to me and it was definitely him, the tall, handsome guy from the streetcar and the movie theatre. "Oh hey. No, I haven't. The bread pudding looks good."

I touched the pan. "Still warm."

He served himself a square then offered me the knife. I couldn't take it by the blade so our hands touched as he gave me the handle. A tiny shudder ran through me and I felt like a kid with a crush. I had to remind myself this guy liked tattooed, leather-jacket-wearing women.

He added a praline and two cookies to his plate. "I missed the service and most of the parade but I heard it was beautiful."

"It really was. I'm sorry you missed it. How did you know Albert?"

"My family lives down the road from here. You?"

"I live down the road from here. Is the rest of your family here?"

"No. I came on my lunch break. That's why I missed everything."

"But the food."

He laughed. "I caught the end." He wiped a crumb from his shirt. "I saw you dancing."

"You did?" I felt suddenly embarrassed, like he'd caught me coming out of the shower.

"Yeah. It was nice. You looked happy."

"At a funeral. Maybe that's not so great."

"It was pretty great."

My face felt hot. Was I blushing? "I'm still getting used to not rolling in misery at a funeral."

"Ah."

He knew I wasn't a native. That was fast. I drove into the skid. "I'm more used to that." I darted my eyes to a woman sitting solemnly.

He looked to her then to his plate. "The one in the purple suit?"

"Yes. She looks sad like a person at a funeral pretty-much everywhere but here."

He laughed. "With that much makeup, how can you tell? It's like a mask. Like is Iron Man sad? I don't know."

A funny observation and a movie reference all in one. I laughed big. Then covered my mouth. Then reminded myself he had a date at that movie.

He smiled at me. "Listen, I was going to get a coffee across the street after this. Would you like to join me? Are you here with people? I didn't even ask."

I reminded myself that plenty of people here were just friendly, and I'd been wrong many times about guys hitting on me. "No. I mean, yes. I'd like to have coffee. Except I really mean tea."

He laughed and threw his plate away. "Come on."

"Wait!"

His smile fell as he stopped.

I laughed. "I didn't mean to scare you. I just, I don't know your name. I don't want to go anywhere with a complete stranger."

"Maybe we're just friends who haven't met yet."

My heart jumped. "My mom says that."

"She sounds smart." He smiled. "I'm Patrick."

"Patrick. I'm Charlotte."

His beautiful mossy green eyes rested on mine as

we shook hands.

We found a table on the sidewalk and tried to ignore the sickening smell of the controlled burn in the Gulf. Albert's growing memorial was just next door. I'd contributed nothing, just took photos and blogged about it. Patrick hadn't added anything either but he thought my blog post might be a contribution of a different sort.

We talked about everything from music to my theory that there's a second Sphinx in Sudan known as the Sunrise Sphinx. My best guess was that it was in Meroe.

He laughed. "That's pretty specific."

"Yeah, I thought about it a lot." I laughed at myself. "Spent so much time researchin' it that I accidentally learned to read hieroglyphs fairly well. But it doesn't help because they used a different language in Meroe and no one has cracked it yet. So, it's just a theory."

"You have a lot of those." He smiled.

I felt warm inside, then pictured the tattooed woman. "Here's one I got wrong. For about five minutes, I thought you were a stalker."

"Because I watched you dance?"

"What? Oh! No, nothing you did. I was helping a friend figure out who was stalking them and you were on the streetcar with us once."

He looked at me like maybe I was the stalker. He didn't look amused.

"It was months ago. Easter. I was looking for a seat and spotted you in the back."

His tone was cautious. "Why do you remember that?"

My stomach tightened. A voice inside me said, "Never die with your mouth full of all the nice things you meant to say." I took a breath. "Because." I chuckled and shook my head. Our eyes connected and I confessed, "Because you're really handsome."

He seemed genuinely taken aback. "That is not what I thought you were going to say."

"Were you hoping for something less... boundary-crossing? I'm not hitting on you. I don't know your situation. Heck, I thought you were a stalker. I don't generally hit on stalkers." I laughed. "Or anyone."

"My situation is that I'm really enjoying meeting you."

Dang. Beautifully played. Either he was awesome or he was a "player" with pretty good game.

"Then I should tell you that I saw you somewhere else after that."

"You did? Are you sure you're not the one stalking me?" He was only half-kidding.

"I know, but it's just a small city, that's all. I saw you at *Iron Man 2* last night."

Patrick smiled. "You like movies?"

I thought about telling him my job. "I love movies."

"My cousin hated it."

His cousin. The tattooed woman was his cousin. "Don't you hate that, when you're having fun at a movie and the people you're with aren't into it?"

"Yeah, but it's pretty rare to find someone with the same taste in movies. If you only liked action movies then we'd only have a little in common. But liking movies is the bottom line."

"Deal breaker?"

He laughed. "Not like a a liar or a cheater deal breaker. More like, Falcons fan deal breaker."

We talked about the Saints, the Super Bowl and the Victory Parade.

He drew the line. "But you're not really a Saints fan until you survive a losing season. True Saints fans are used to loving them when they sucked, when we called 'em the "Aints" and people at the games wore paper bags over their heads in shame."

"I'm used to losing. I have one of those jobs where for every time you get a win, there are dozens of failures. And you have to keep believin' against all evidence to the contrary."

He smiled. "My job can be like that too. I guess a lot of people have that."

"Whether you're a salesperson or Babe Ruth."

Patrick let the waitress refill his cup. He wasn't in any hurry. "You know something about everything."

"We learn by paying attention and we pay the most attention to things that fascinate us. I'm just easily fascinated."

I felt myself liking Patrick more than was reasonable for a stranger. I thought about the fortune teller in Jackson Square. Patrick seemed to be my age. That said, I'd thought Tom was my age for a couple of weeks before I discovered he was ten years younger than I was. After almost two decades of surrounding myself with the "perpetually young" of L.A., the grey at his temples had thrown me. Patrick was fully salt-and-pepper and struck me as mature. Maybe the fortune teller had been wrong about my guy being older. Patrick seemed to be a great communicator. That was what Stella said had made her think he'd be older.

Given that we'd been letting the day fly by at a coffee shop, Patrick didn't seem to be much of a workaholic. Plus, Stella was just a lady with a lot of scarves we'd randomly picked from many others offering totally different futures.

A couple pushing a stroller stopped in front of Albert's memorial and tried to find a spot to add something. The husband leaned over and looked at some of the photos and notes. The wife pointed to a note and they shared a laugh.

Patrick asked me about the service and I told him about the crowd and about the Bishop saying it was a "celebrity funeral."

He laughed. "Was there a red carpet?"

"I was just glad it was a totally organic community coming-together. No publicists or party promoters involved."

"What's a party promoter?"

"It's a job. It's... " Maybe Patrick would be excited I was in movies and maybe he would make me feel like "other." Or maybe he wouldn't care and I'd have that now-familiar feeling that I was dragging L.A. into conversations like the memory of an old boyfriend. "You know what? Who cares."

"To heck with party promoters. They're all jerks anyway."

I laughed.

The waitress brought the check and Patrick paid it.

"Thank you." I smiled at him and my breath got shallow. "The Bishop said this cool thing about talking to strangers. He was talking about how so many of us were people who'd met Albert by talking to a stranger and how Albert did that all the time."

"What'd he say?"

"He said you never know who you'll meet."

He smiled. "No, you never do."

He had to be a player. How else could he keep saying things that made me feel happy and known? He was probably like the fortune teller, observant and calculating.

"I've gotta go." I picked up my backpack and dusted off the bottom. "I didn't realize how late it's getting."

He looked at his phone for the time. "Oh! I really let the day get away from me."

We both stood. He put his hand out. "I liked meeting you Charlotte."

"I liked meeting you too."

"After all that stalking."

I laughed. "I shoulda never have told you. The only thing worse than revealing that I had an eye-crush on you was clearing up that you had no memory of me."

"No, but those days are over." He smiled a little.

He had to be a player. He was way too dreamy.

"Listen, you said you like to do things for your blog. Would you like to tour a historic home in the French Quarter tomorrow?"

Tomorrow? Didn't he know players aren't supposed to appear too interested? "Tomorrow?" I did like that he'd listened about my blog and was being supportive.

"It's a work thing. I get a free pass if you'd like to meet me in the Quarter after five."

I resisted making a plus-one joke. "Yeah. Can I take photos?"

"Yeah. I can probably get you an interview with one of the preservationists if you want."

My eyes went wide. "I've never done an interview. Why haven't I ever asked anyone anything? It honestly never even occurred to me. That's crazy."

He laughed. "It's me. I was talking about me."

I laughed with him. "Oh! Yes. Sure, I'd love to interview you."

"I haven't read your blog so I didn't realize it was going to be something new."

I was used to giving people an "out." It was one of Carter's favorite things about me. Clarence thought it made me "cool." "No pressure. I always try to stay open to a better idea but I love my blog the way it is. I'm good either way."

He wrote the address of the tour on the back of his card and handed it too me. The more I wanted to hug him, the more I was certain it was better to walk away with a wave. "See you tomorrow."

"See you then."

I couldn't wait to get home and call Sofia. I could still hear Patrick's laugh and see his beautiful mossy eyes.

The chandelier was dormant as I grabbed a landline and dialed. The air in the house smelled just as bad as it did outside, the reek of burning chemicals. "Sofia! I'm so glad you're home."

She sounded breathless. "Hey! You sound good. Did you get another part?"

"I may have met someone."

She laughed. "That was fast. They really are a dime a dozen."

I told her about Patrick, about meeting him at the funeral and how he'd watched me dance. She liked that he wanted to see me again right away.

"But he could be playing me. That could be his play, the 'I'm crazy about you' play where you start wondering if they're just crazy in general."

She started laughing. "Yeah, maybe he's just tricking you by being polite and a good listener."

"It's happened before."

She was laughing harder. "Maybe he'll trick you into having a wonderful time and falling in love."

I tried not to laugh but she was infectious. "You're making it sound like I'm paranoid, but it's not paranoia if they really are all trying to play you."

She was cracking herself up. "Maybe he'll trick you into living happily ever after with him."

"It's not funny." I couldn't stop laughing.

"It's pretty funny. You're so used to jerks, you don't remember what it would look like if you just went on a nice date with a nice guy. Except Tom."

"Dime a dozen," I teased.

"People are nice to each other for no reason there. Maybe it's normal to go on nice dates when you actually want the other person to like you. Stranger things have happened."

I laughed. "The Saints won the Super Bowl!"

Sofia always had a way of reminding me that the improbable was totally possible. I missed her, but I was glad I was building a new life in a city where Albert was a "celebrity" because he'd been so friendly and kind to so many.

I opened my laptop and checked my blog stats. Two new subscribers. I clicked the link to see their email addresses. PCollins. I pulled the business card from my backpack and turned it in the light. Patrick Collins. He was definitely not worried about appearing too interested.

I checked my email and found one from Taffy. "Eunoe's mother was named Lottie. There's no name for her mother or father. Let us know if you figure anything out." There was an attachment. I clicked it and the photo popped open. Wearing a Saints bow, Jojo looked up at the camera with Pryor eyes.

I searched for the computer file with the photos from Julia's phone. Mom, Julia and Bryan smiled in a shot I had taken. Julia posed with Trevor in another. I clicked on a photo of the bill of sale and scanned the writing. "Sold a certain negro woman named Lottie."

Should I tell Taffy and Chiffon? I had no idea if it was the same Lottie. Maybe that was a popular name in the 1800's. Maybe it was nothing, though it might help explain how Sassy came to have a chandelier from my family's plantation. If that bill of sale was even from my family plantation. If the chandelier was originally ours and Lottie was the same Lottie that was with our family back then, she would've gone with my ancestor, Lily, and they would both have had a story of traveling with a chandelier. That made sense.

That crazy chandelier. Was Mama Heck doing her job as "The Protector?" Did she want me digging into her family secrets or was she warning me off of the topic? The fortune teller had said I was The Protector and that I knew what she was talking about. Was the chandelier asking me to protect it like Sofia thought? Tom said the ghost protects a family secret. If I was "The Protector," shouldn't I know what that secret was? I didn't even know if there was a secret. And hadn't Stella said to be careful asking questions you don't want the answers to? What if my family did awful things to Sassy's family? Would I want to know? Would Taffy and Chiffon?

Focus. Lottie. Mama T. Short for Carlotta? Charlotte? That would be funny. There was no one in the *Iliad* by any of those names. Maybe it was nothing, a coincidence. It was perfectly reasonable that there would be a Lottie at the Wells Plantation and another Lottie who had Mama Eunoe... who ended up with a chandelier from the Wells Plantation? It had to be the same Lottie, didn't it? Maybe Taffy and Chiffon wouldn't want to know my family owned their family for generations. I wasn't sure I wanted to know. Maybe it was better not to ask.

I thought about Taffy and Chiffon. I tried to put myself in their shoes. I'm a twin found in a laundromat who's raised by an amazing mother. I would want to know my birth mother. That made sense. Would I want to know the history of the mother who raised me but wasn't my blood? Lottie's story wasn't their bloodline but it was their heritage. Those breadcrumbs they left to find each other might have been to safeguard their family from my family, but we all deserved to know.

Was that our family secret? That our family had owned Sassy's family? I wasn't sure what the first initials scratched into the chandelier socket were but the second initial was "W." Wells. Sassy's chandelier was our family's chandelier, right? But there wasn't much shame in people owning slaves back then. Mama Eunoe was born a slave. My family's slave? Had she left with Lily and the chandelier?

What if it was a different secret? Maybe it was their identities. Lily and Mama Eunoe might've traveled under different names if they were running away from Lily's father. Maybe the chandelier had to always hang to hide the etched-initials. That made sense. That made a lot of sense.

But I still didn't know why the Wells' symbol was on Dad's pipe. Or the flask at May Baily's.

My own family breadcrumbs were calling to me.

APPENDIX

These people and places mentioned in the book are real and open for business as of this publishing. For more information on anything mentioned in this book, use the search tool in LAtoNOLA (latonola.com), the blog upon which many of the book's recollections are based.

Bacchanal
http://www.bacchanalwine.com

Bar Tonique
http://bartonique.com

Bryan Batt
http://www.bryanbatt.com

Bayona
http://www.bayona.com

Jeff Beck
http://www.jeffbeck.com

Bonerama
http://www.boneramabrass.com

Big Chief Monk Boudreaux
http://www.bigchiefmonk.com

Cafe du Monde
http://www.cafedumonde.com

Chris Owens
http://www.chrisowensclub.net/pages/home.html

Commander's Palace
http://www.commanderspalace.com

Court of Two Sisters
http://www.courtoftwosisters.com

Crepes a la Cart
http://crepecaterer.com

Dancing Man 504
https://www.facebook.com/Dancing-Man-504-239176338346/

Design Within Reach
http://www.dwr.com

Dirty Dozen Brass Band
http://www.dirtydozenbrass.com

Evergreen Plantation
http://evergreenplantation.org

Fleurty Girl
http://www.fleurtygirl.net

Forever New Orleans
https://www.facebook.com/foreverneworleans

French Quarter Fest
http://fqfi.org

Garden District Book Shop
http://www.gardendistrictbookshop.com

Gravity A
http://www.gravitya.com

Harry's Corner Bar
https://www.facebook.com/Harrys-Corner-139022506152999/

Hazelnut New Orleans
http://www.hazelnutneworleans.com

IMDb (International Movie Database)
http://www.imdb.com

Billy Iuso
http://www.billyiuso.com

Jazz Fest - New Orleans Jazz & Heritage Festival
http://www.nojazzfest.com

Junco Partners
http://www.juncopartners.com

Doreen Ketchens (clarinet player)
http://www.doreensjazz.com

B.B. King
http://www.bbking.com

May Baily's Place
http://www.dauphineorleans.com/nightlife

Mother-in-Law Lounge - Kermit's Treme Mother-in-Law Lounge
http://www.kermitstrememotherinlawlounge.com

Muriel's Jackson Square
http://muriels.com

M.S. Rau
https://www.rauantiques.com

Sabai
http://www.sabaijewelry.com

Sonny Landreth
http://www.sonnylandreth.com

Christine Miller - Two Chicks Walking Tours
http://www.twochickswalkingtours.com

Van Morrison
http://www.vanmorrison.com/splash/

Mystikal
https://www.facebook.com/itsmystikal/

Anders Osborne
http://www.andersosborne.com

Margie Perez
https://www.facebook.com/MargiePerezSings

Prytania Theatre
http://prytaniatheatreneworleans.com

The Pussyfooters
http://www.pussyfooters.org

Rebirth Brass Band
http://www.rebirthbrassband.com

The Roots of Music
http://therootsofmusic.org

Rouses
https://shop.rouses.com

Kermit Ruffins
https://www.facebook.com/kermitruffinsnola/

The Neville Brothers
http://www.nevilles.com

The New Orleans Saints
http://www.neworleanssaints.com

The Singing Oak ("Bing Bong Tree")
https://www.youtube.com/watch?v=Mcwiy5TKQ6M

 Rhonda Smith (Jeff Beck's bassist)
http://rhondasmith.com

Soul Rebels
http://thesoulrebels.com

Tanya and Dorise (violinist and guitarist)
http://tanyandorise.com

TBC Brass Band
http://www.tbcbrassband.com/TBC_Brass_Band/Home.html

Tipitina's
http://www.tipitinas.com

HBO's Treme
http://www.hbo.com/treme

Trombone Shorty
http://www.tromboneshorty.com

101 Runners
https://www.facebook.com/101runners/

1850 House
http://louisianastatemuseum.org/museums/1850-house/

These people are gone but you can read more about them on my blog,
LAtoNOLA.

Albert Joseph
https://latonola.wordpress.com/2010/08/05/r-i-p-albert-joseph-jackson-
the-moses-of-magazine-street/

Claudia Speicher
https://latonola.wordpress.com/2014/01/30/remembering-claudia-
speicher/

ABOUT THE AUTHOR

Best known for her role as Leonardo DiCaprio's sister in Quentin Tarantino's *Django Unchained*, Laura Cayouette has acted in over 40 films including *Now You See Me*, *Kill Bill* and *Enemy of the State*. Television appearances include *True Detective*, *Friends* and an award winning episode of *The Larry Sanders Show*.

Laura earned a Master's Degree in creative writing and English literature at the University of South Alabama where she was awarded Distinguished Alumni 2014. She currently resides in New Orleans.

Website: lauracayouette.com
Twitter: @KnowSmallParts
Facebook: http://bit.ly/1VxJIvr

48951773R00146

Made in the USA
San Bernardino, CA
10 May 2017